THE VOICE OF REVENGE

MOLLIN MUZUVA

AuthorHouse™ UK
1663 Liberty Drive
Bloomington, IN 47403 USA
www.authorhouse.co.uk
Phone: 0800.197.4150

Published by AuthorHouse   10/30/18

ISBN: 978-1-5462-9143-5 (sc)
ISBN: 978-1-5462-9142-8 (e)

CONTENTS

ACKNOWLEDGEMENT

I would like to thank Christiana Mandizha my Daughter In Law for helping me to Edit this book and I am very grateful for her contribution in making my dream come true as this is my first Fiction Book and I was doubting whether Fiction was my thing but Christiana was very encouraging and made me feel that I should go ahead with Publishing The Voice of Revenge as she quite enjoyed reading the Manuscript and thought it was going to be enjoyed by many other people reading it.

INTRODUCTION

This is the story of Methuselah Tyke, who was born in Sarowe village, about 250 kilometres from Gaborone in Botswana. Born on 17 July 1939, he was an only child. His grandparents brought him up because he became an orphan at age twelve.

Methuselah was determined to seek revenge for the death of his parents. Chief Muyabwo gave his parents a death sentence after they were accused of bewitching one of the villager's daughters, Sarah. The accusations were unjustified and could not be conclusive.

Chief Muyabwo ruled Sarowe Village for fifty years and was well-known for his callousness. Pitiless as he was, he would not try to rationalise complaints from villagers. He took any issues regarding witchcraft very seriously. Villagers were put to task when there were any reports involving witchcraft. Also, he had a weakness of taking other people's wives.

Anyone who knew Chief Muyabwo was aware of his cruelty and poor treatment of villagers. He was quite a powerful person with his own police, and he had the right to make his own judgements about villagers. He had been given the powers by the government. He was paid by the government for doing the job, but what the government did not realise was that he had taken law into his own hands.

Villagers were living in fright all the time because of his terror. Chief Muyabwo's sons threatened most people in the village. He felt empowered because of his police, his security men, and his sons.

The chief had people he favoured most in the village, and he would not allow anything to happen to them. Sarah's parents got on very well with the chief. If anything went wrong with the people he liked, the chief would do whatever it took to make sure they were happy with his judgement.

The chief did not quite like Methuselah's parents for reasons known only to him. Methuselah's parents knew that the chief did not like them. Sithu and Bayeme knew they had not done anything to upset the chief, and therefore they kept to themselves.

CHAPTER 1

Family Life

Sithu lived in Sarowe village and was happily married. She was twenty-nine years of age, thin as a rake, and five feet tall. She was light in complexion and always had a lovely smile. She had long, beautiful black hair that was always tied at the back to keep it nice and tidy. She was well-known for being kind and friendly. But Sithu also had weaknesses. Although she was kind and generous, whenever she fell out with someone, she reclaimed whatever she had given to them. Further, whenever she baked some wheat bread, she dunked it in her tea.

Bayeme, her husband, was thirty years old, about six feet tall, and well built. His complexion was as dark as coal. He was not very good-looking and had a face not even a mother could love. He had a big nose, and his long teeth protruded from his mouth. His speech was a bit impeded due to the structure of his teeth. He had kinky black hair, which at times looked like wires coming out of his head. He was not as friendly to people as his wife, but he was dedicated to his family. He liked his pint and drank it like water. It appeared he would drink out his senses because he would fight each time he had a drink.

Their only son, Methuselah, was born on 17 October 1939. His looks were good, and he turned a lot of heads when he walked down the road. His complexion was light, like his mum's. Methuselah's hair was kinky and black, just like his dad's. Sithu, Bayeme, and Methuselah had very mysterious brown eyes which seemed to hold untold secrets within them. A person could get lost if one gazed into them for too long. Because Sithu was small and slim, she looked nice in whatever type of clothes she wore.

Bayeme, who was big, had large hands which seemed to flap about, as though trying to escape from the sleeves of his shirts.

They were a very close family and spent most of their time together working outside. Methuselah was breastfed until he was two years old because they believed breast milk to be best for him. Methuselah was such a big child, and Sithu said that by age two, he actually knelt on the floor to breastfeed because he was too big to put on her lap! Besides breast milk, he also had porridge made with maize meal mixed with some milk. Other supplementary meals were mashed potatoes with some soup.

Methuselah was not a difficult child to please as long as he had eaten and had his favourite towel, which he'd had from birth. That towel was magic and kept Methuselah content. His parents wondered what was so special about the towel. He would carry it around inside and outside the house, sniffing it like a dog. One day his mother felt that it was too torn apart for her son. She decided to put it in the dogs' kennel for them to lie on. When four-year-old Methuselah followed his mother to the kennel to feed the dogs, he saw his towel in the kennel and started crying for his towel. "Mum, please get my towel."

"You can't use it now. The dogs have been lying on it."

"No, Mum, please. I want it back."

In the end, his mum could not silence him until she let him go inside the kennel to get the towel. One of the dogs raised a lip as he pulled the towel from underneath it, but Methuselah did not care. As soon as he got the towel, he started sniffing it straightaway. Sithu said she could not stop laughing; the dog's grin meant it also enjoyed the comfort he got from lying on the towel. His mother took the towel from Methuselah and washed it before letting her son use it.

The family had two beautiful, black, male Alsatian dogs, Sam and Poky. They were Methuselah's best friends. He played with them all the time, more than he played with the other kids. He fed them with whatever was left from what the family ate. One day there were no leftovers, and so they cooked something quick for them. Sam and Poky refused to eat because it was not as tasty. Both tipped the food onto the ground.

Now and again, when his mother was not looking, Methuselah shared whatever he was eating with the dogs. One day he shared his boiled potato with Sam, and the dog ate the whole potato. Angrily, Methuselah bit Sam on his nose. Thank God Sam was not a vicious dog; otherwise, Methuselah would have been in trouble.

At the age of six, Methuselah started school at Bait Primary School, a five-minute walk from his home. The first week was a bit of a struggle because he did not want to part with his mother. Sithu had to take him to school daily until he got used to the idea. The teachers reported he cried his eyes out the first day because he wanted his mum and his special blanket. During the first week at school, the teachers allowed him to take the blanket into class because without it, he sobbed his eyes out. No one could calm him.

In the morning, Sithu struggled to get Methuselah up. "Methuselah! Wake up, darling. Time to get ready for school."

"Mum, please give me two more minutes. Just two more minutes, and I will be OK."

She tried ten minutes later, and he was in a deep sleep again. He was her only child, and so she did not want to upset him. Sithu sometimes tried to wake him up much earlier because it took longer for him to finally get up. She also packed him some food to eat during break; it was nothing much, just a boiled egg, potatoes, and some relish. On good days, she baked some wheat bread, and he would have that with milk.

After a few weeks, Methuselah had settled in and started enjoying school a lot. He reported to his parents what he learned at school. He made a few friends at school: Luke, John, and Mark. He was as bright as a button and interested in all his schoolwork. Methuselah was amongst those at the top of the class in every subject.

CHAPTER 2

Lifestyle

In the summer, the village looked deserted because everyone was busy in the field. Like the other villagers, Methuselah's family depended a lot on peasant farming to add to Bayeme's wages. They woke up at dawn; though it was still slightly dark, one could still manage to do some work. As soon as the sun started to rise, Bayeme left the field to get ready for work, and Methuselah got ready for school. Saturdays were the best because the whole family worked together the entire day in the field. They only had a break when they went home for their breakfast and lunch. His mother was always busy. She went home to prepare the family's meals as well as work in the field. Bayeme and his son ate large portions at mealtime because they were always as hungry as wolves.

In the field, they grew maize, wheat, cotton, pumpkins, rye, sunflowers, and groundnuts. Most of these were used for their own use, but they sold the rest. In winter and spring, Sithu concentrated on gardening. It appeared she had green fingers because yields were great in the garden and fields.

Sithu was always hard-working, and she expected her son to be likewise. "Methuselah, we want you to be a hard-working and independent boy," his mother told him whenever she woke him up. "Life is full of surprises, my son. You never know what's around the corner. Nothing comes when you are sleeping. You always have to sweat for whatever you get in life. Your dad and I have always worked hard because nothing comes easily in life. You have to do likewise if you are to survive in society."

"OK, Mum. I will try my best."

Methuselah was a very sensible boy by then and never sulked when woken up too early. He appreciated that his parents meant well in training him the hard way. Although he was an only child, he was never spoiled. His parents believed Methuselah should be fully independent with everything at an early age.

At nine years old, Methuselah learned to be a responsible boy. He helped his parents wherever he could. He helped with cleaning the house and gardening. He used a wheelbarrow to fetch wood from the forest for his mother.

The family lived in round huts as old as the hills. They were built of wood, sealed with mud, and thatched with grass. They had two separate huts apart from the kitchen, which were used as bedrooms. They slept on the mud floor because they had no beds. Methuselah's dad made his family's furniture from wood. Sithu made the kitchen to her liking. They used fire for cooking, and the fireplace was made from mud. Iron fixtures were applied to the top to suit the odd-shaped pots she used.

The family had a dinner made from maize meal, served with vegetables from the garden or mice. The mice were always roasted on the fire just before the family went to bed. They were left by the fire to dry with heat from the dead fire, and by morning, they were very crispy. After school, Methuselah went round the fields to dig the mice out of the ground.

Weekends and special occasions were when they cooked maize meal or some rice with chicken. The family always had tea and some sweet potatoes, or tea with brown rice mixed with peanut butter, or tea with some wheat bread for breakfast.

They also had a herd of cattle and a few goats, as well as a brood of chickens. It appeared that for meat, they had no problems. Sithu would milk their cows during the week, and then her husband and Methuselah would take over during weekends. They had enough chickens and so would have chicken whenever they fancied meat. The chickens laid enough eggs for the family, and they could spare some to sell or give to close friends. Goats and cattle were only slaughtered on family gatherings or sold for a bit of cash. As far as herding the cattle was concerned, villagers would take turns to herd them. Sintu's family's turn came once every month on a weekend, when Bayeme and Methuselah would be available.

In the evenings, the family would sit in their little hut and tell each other fairy tales. His parents used to tell him all the old stories of what used to happen when they were growing up. However, if Methuselah had some homework, he would go to his room to do his homework.

Some weekends Methuselah would play with other village kids, and they would play hide and seek. It had to be a good day, when it was not raining and was not cold. He used to enjoy playing with other children very much because he was an only child, and as such he had no one to play with at home.

One evening as the children were playing hide and seek, an eight-year-old girl went into hiding, and they could not find her. They looked in all the possible places they thought she could be hiding but could not find her. The girl's name was Felicia. All the other children started searching for her and calling her.

"Felicia, where are you? Please come out. The game is over now."

"I bet you can hear us but are trying to be difficult."

"We will not play with you anymore! I mean it."

"You are very naughty. If I call your mum, you will get a good hiding."

After a thirty-minute search, they had to alert the parents, who were not very happy. They searched inside Felicia's bedroom and found her fast asleep.

"What on earth are you doing sleeping in your bedroom, when we are busy looking for you?" one kid asked.

Felicia had gone into hiding in her bedroom, but in the process she had fallen asleep. All parents who were present during the search warned the kids not to play that game again, or else they would not be allowed to play together in the evening.

CHAPTER 3

Visit to Biet Bridge

The day was bright on 10 October 1949. Sithu, Bayeme, and Methuselah set off to visit Sithu's family. The whole family were happy as larks, looking forward to seeing all their loved ones in Beit Bridge. They took all they thought was required for the journey.

They boarded a bus going to Biet Bridge at 9 a.m. from Botswana. Then from Biet Bridge, they boarded a bus to the rural area of Ndlovu. The rest of the family were in the fields because they were not expecting them. They walked to the fields, which was not far. Sintu's parents were quite thrilled to see them arriving. There was so much screaming of delight and welcome.

"Hello, Mum and Dad. We thought we would give you a surprise visit this morning," Sithu said with enthusiasm.

"Good to see you all. What a nice surprise!" Sithu's father said.

"Oh, my word. Methuselah has grown so much, eh? Methuselah, you are a big boy now," Sithu's mother said.

Methuselah replied, "Grandma! You look good, and you seem not to be ageing much. I love you very much, Grandma, and I missed you so much."

"How about the crops in the field? Do you think it's going to be a good harvest?" Bayeme asked. He was interested in agriculture.

"The rains have been very good this year, and we are expecting the yields to be good," Grandma confirmed.

Following the welcome, they walked back home. In no time, Grandma started cooking. She first boiled the kettle and made some tea with some wheat bread. Meanwhile, she had put some biltong on the fire for lunch, which she would serve with vegetables and brown rice. For the evening meal, Sithu's mum insisted that a goat be slaughtered for that day, and then cattle would be slaughtered the following day. They could enjoy these meats together. After about an hour, they sent for Sithu's brother and sister, who lived in the next village.

Violet and Denise brought their families along, and they were so pleased to see Sithu and her family. They had not seen each other for two years, because Sarowe was a long distance away.

When the food was ready, they gathered together to eat and drink to celebrate their getting together. Later, they all thanked Grandma for the nice meal.

"It has been a long time since we last saw each other, so we had to make an effort," Sithu said. "I know everyone is busy, but it's also important to meet as a family."

"Yes, Sithu, you are right. We appreciate your coming," Denise agreed.

"When you see how the kids have grown, then you can actually see that it has been too long," Violet said.

After that discussion, they decided to sing a gospel song. Then they had a short prayer together to thank God for reuniting them together when everyone was in good health and alive. Later, Denise, his dad, Bayeme, and Methuselah went to look for the goat, taking some knives and some dishes to put the meat on. When they finished slaughtering the goat, then it was time for the women to clean the inner parts of the goat and start cooking.

They continued to tell each other what had been happening during the years they had been apart. Sithu and Bayeme were surprised to see how Violet and Denise's children had grown. They could tell Sithu's parents had aged a bit but were still strong as oxen. Their home was well maintained, and they still had good harvests.

Sithu and Bayeme spent most of their holiday helping in the fields and at the house. There were quite heavy rainfalls most of the time they were in Biet Bridge. During the times when it was not raining, they would go around the village, seeing all those whom they were related to and some old friends.

They spent about two weeks at Sithu's home, and then they had to go back to Sarowe. They had a great time with Sithu's family. Before they were due to go back, they decided to also spend at least one night with Denise and family, and then with Violet and family. On Sunday morning, they woke up early to get ready to go back to Sarowe.

"I want to spend more time with Grandma and Granddad but I have to go to school," Methuselah said.

"Never mind, sweetheart. There is more time in the future," his grandma said.

"Well, Grandma, it seems the time is now. You never can tell about tomorrow."

They bade farewell and went to the station to board their transport to go back home. Within three hours, they arrived home. On arrival, Sithu and Bayeme started organising everything for work the following day. As for Methuselah, it was time to make sure his school bags and his homework were put together before school.

CHAPTER 4

Fight at School

It was Friday afternoon, and all the kids had to stay longer for sports. The day was nice and was not too hot, a good day for sports. Methuselah and his friends were quite excited because they were good at sports. Sarah, Bijou's daughter, was very good at running, and she would normally win, as did Methuselah.

When it was time to start running, all the children gathered at the ground as usual. The teachers started organising the children into groups. It just so happened that Methuselah and Sarah were in the same group. Sarah normally was unhappy about competing with Methuselah because she felt threatened. They started off with the 100-metre run. Methuselah and Sarah both ran for the 100 meters. When they were told to go, everybody started cheering.

"Come on, Methuselah! You are almost there," said Paul, one of Methuselah's friends.

It appeared that the more his friends cheered him on, the faster he ran. As he reached the winning point, he was leading, and Sarah and the others were still very far from catching him. Methuselah won! Sarah started crying as if she was jealous of Methuselah winning. The teachers could see that Sarah was unhappy about why they'd decided to let the girls to compete with the boys. Normally girls would compete with other girls, and boys would compete with other boys. Overall the sports day went well, and everyone was happy with how the afternoon went—except Sarah.

When the sports were all over, the rest of the kids took their belongings and started walking home. Sarah went ahead of Methuselah and his friends, and she waited for him at a point when all his friends would be gone. As soon as she saw him, she started verbally attacking him.

"You think you are clever. Well, today I am going to fix you, you son of a bitch."

"Sarah, there is no need for all that bitchiness," Methuselah said.

"I have been meaning to hit you for a long time. Today I am going to teach you a lesson."

"Please, Sarah. Just leave me alone. I will not fight a woman."

"Nonsense. What do you think you are?"

Before he knew it, Methuselah was hit on his nose, and it started bleeding. As soon as Methuselah saw blood, he got as mad as a hornet. He could not understand why Sarah was being so angry with him. He then hit her back, and she fell to the ground, crying loudly. The other kids had to intervene to end the fight.

"I am going to report you to my mum and dad, Methuselah. You think you are clever. My dad will hit you the next time he sees you."

"Well, you started the fight for no apparent reason. I don't care who you are going to tell, but you should know that you don't start a fight when you can't handle it."

When Sarah got home, she was still sobbing. As soon as she got home, her parents went ballistic. "What? Sarah is crying. What is going on?" Bijou asked anxiously.

"Methuselah beat me when I was coming from school."

"Why would he do that?"

"I started a fight."

"Did he hurt you?"

"No. He hit me, and I fell on the ground."

"But, Sarah, you should not fight with boys."

Her parents comforted her and made sure she was not hurt. Her dad said he would talk to Methuselah's parents the following day because it was getting late.

Meanwhile, Methuselah's parents were not happy when they saw him with some blood on his shirt. They asked him what had happened, and he narrated the whole story to them.

"Are you feeling OK with yourself?"

"Yes, Mum. You know Sarah is only a girl; she can't hurt me."

"But you have to be careful. You know Sarah's dad is the chief's cousin."

Sithu took Methuselah, cleaned the blood on his nose, and put away the shirt for washing. They gave him his supper and asked him to go to bed early for some rest. Later in their bedroom, they wondered how Sarah's parents were going to take it. They thought it was very common for children to fight, and it took someone unreasonable to take the fight seriously. It appeared no one was hurt, and so they should be OK. On that note they went to sleep.

CHAPTER 5

Tragedy at Sarowe

On Monday morning, 30 October 1952, Sarah went to school as usual. She spent the whole day with no complaints of pain or a headache. She had her supper as usual with her parents; her sister Tina, who was ten; and her brother Leonard, who was eight. Sarah was twelve years old, and she was quite grown for her age.

After supper, the kids were all playing well, and no one had complained of anything. For some reason, Sarah was extraordinarily happy that particular day, cracking jokes with other kids and laughing all the time. It seemed as if she was saying goodbye to the other children. Sarah managed to do her homework, said goodnight to her family, and then went to sleep. That particular night, she gave her mother, father, sister, and brother a hug and a kiss before she went to sleep, which was unusual for her.

On Tuesday morning, 31 November 1952, Bijou went into Sarah's room to find she was unresponsive when trying to wake her up.

"Sarah! Sarah! Oh, my God! She is not responding." Bijou started crying.

"Is she in a deep sleep?" Bernard asked as he rushed in.

"I don't think so. Bernard, she has not done this before."

"We'd better rush her to the clinic and see whether there is anything they can do."

"Oh, oh! What am I going to do?" Bijou continued crying.

Bernard quickly carried Sarah on his back whilst Bijou followed with the other kids. They got to the clinic in no time, but when they arrived, Sarah was pronounced dead. Bijou and Bernard went hysterical, and no one could control their crying. The nurses tried to console them, but it was difficult.

"Sarah was healthy and very active. I just cannot understand this," Bernard said.

"Sarah! Sarah! Oh, my girl! She left us without saying goodbye."

"She died peacefully in her sleep. What a way to go."

"Last night she was so happy, playing with the other kids. She appeared to be the happiest child."

They were advised what to do next in terms of making funeral arrangements. After that, they went back home. Most people learned about the tragic death of Sarah and gathered together to mourn her. The chief and his family were present from the day it happened until the day she was buried. Funeral arrangements were made, and she was laid to rest the following day.

"Someone is going to pay for this. It must be something to do with witchcraft. It can't be a natural death," Chief Muyabwo said.

Methuselah's parents, Sithu and Bayeme, were also at the funeral. They were shocked by the sad loss of Sarah. They both liked Sarah because she was a very nice girl and had a lot of respect for adults.

After the funeral, Sithu and Bayeme went back to their home and were still disturbed by the news.

"What a way to go for a lovely girl like Sarah," Sithu said.

"Well, when it's your time to die, you have no choice," Bayeme commented.

As Sithu and Bayeme sympathised with Sarah's death, little did they know that they would end up being suspects. They were genuine with everything they said about the death and were not expecting any blame to be placed on them.

On the other hand, if it was not for Toutswe, the witch doctor, Bijou and Bernard would not have yet been conclusive about the cause of their daughter's death. They could have been suspicious of witchcraft but might not have suspected Methuselah's parents.

The villagers were totally in the dark and could not have suspected any witchcraft amongst each other. Obviously what they were aware of was that Chief Muyabwo would put to task anyone accused of witchcraft. Prior to the time of their memorial, Chief Muyabwo had charged two other villagers accused of bewitching two other families who had suffered a similar loss. As long as there was unexpected death, Chief Muyabwo would suspect witchcraft.

14

CHAPTER 6

Death Inquest

Two weeks after Sarah's death, her parents went to find out the cause of death from a witch doctor. The witch doctor operated from a spirit realm and was believed to be shown the cause of death. During that time, people were still very traditional in most parts of Africa, and they trusted in any findings from witch doctors, believing them to be true and reliable.

Bijou and Bernard woke up early one Saturday morning and walked about ten miles to Toutswe's place. Toutswe was considered the most famous witch doctor within the Sarowe area. He was six feet eight inches tall, ugly, and as bald as a coot. Chief Muyabwo trusted him very much and believed him to be as wise as an owl. Toutswe was married but had no children for reasons known only to him and his wife.

As Bijou and Bernard arrived, Toutswe's wife met them at the entrance. They informed her of their reason for coming, and she took them to the small hut from where Toutswe was operating. She told them to take off their shoes before entering—a sign of respect to the spirit medium. Also, they had to clap their hands when entering, because that was another way of respecting the spirit medium.

When they entered the hut, they saw Toutswe on a traditional mat made from cattle skin. He was wearing just a skirt made from animal skin and had beads around his neck, hands, and feet. He had no shoes on because the spirit medium lived in the olden days when there were no shoes. He had a long beard and dreadlocks. Anything accepted within the spirit realm had to be old-fashioned. For instance, Toutswe would drink from a calabash because glasses were not there during his ancestors' lifetime.

Toutswe glared at them when they walked in, and he started shaking his whole body. That was a sign to show that he was filled with his ancestors' spirit. He had a special contraption which looked like a mirror, and he would look through that for any information from the spirit realm.

"Epina! Epina! Epina! Epina! What do I see here? What do I see here? Oh, I see a deep pit! A very dark pit indeed. Ha! Whose idea was it? Whose idea was it? Tell me! Whose idea was it?" He paced up and down the skin mat as though all of a sudden it had become too hot to stand on. Then he finally turned and glared at them again. In a low tone that bordered on accusation, he said, "The spirit informs me that there has been a tragic event in your family. True or false?"

"True," Sarah's parents concurred.

"My ancestor's spirit is grieving with you. I am sorry about your loss. Who died in your family?"

"Our daughter died mysteriously, my lord. She was a very healthy child, and unfortunately she died in her sleep. She went to sleep, and when we went to her room the following morning, she was no more," Bernard explained.

"As I am looking through this mirror, I am being shown that your enemy lives right in your midst; a few paces from your dwellings. Did you quarrel with them before the death of the deceased?"

"Not quite, but Sarah had a fight at school with Methuselah not long ago."

"Well, there you are! Why then have you bothered to disturb me? So you can see where it started from?" Toutswe nodded his head and spat out some dark sap from the root that he was violently chewing. "You must thank your ancestors, who have been preventing this from happening. These people have been trying for a long time to cause confusion and unrest within your family. Further, from what I am being shown, it seems your daughter did not stand a chance. I see a big shadow standing by her and two goblins before her death. Oh, what did this poor soul do to deserve such an unhappy ending? The shadow overwhelmed her, and the goblins used her body for supper! Oh, what did the poor soul do to deserve this? You can never understand this; these things operate in the spirit realm." Toutswe's eyes were now transfixed at his trembling guests.

"As I am in the spirit, I actually hear the squeaking voices of the goblins telling Sarah the day she died that they were not going to go with their stomachs empty. She had to die; there was no choice. Your enemies had already made the decision!"

Toutswe could have gone on for a long time because he claimed to be shown so many things of the spiritual realm. Bijou and Bernard were devastated and heartbroken as Toutswe claimed to be shown all that had happened when their daughter had died. Bijou could not stop crying because it all seemed real.

"Don't cry. I am going to make sure these intruders pay, and pay dearly! I am going to give you some roots and herbs, with instructions to follow to prevent this from happening again."

At the end, Toutswe was explicit that the people who were responsible for their daughter's death were Sithu and Bayeme. He advised them to report it to Chief Muyabwo as soon as possible. Toutswe said he was prepared to testify his findings before the chief. He knew the chief would be interested in anything to do with witchcraft in his village.

He gave them different roots and herbs as he had promised; they were to use them as soon as they got home. The first one was in powdered form, and they had to put some burning ashes on a metal tray and sprinkle the powder on the burning ashes. The whole family would inhale the smoke while covered in the same blanket. All the doors and the windows had to be closed. He said the powdered herbal stuff was to chase away all the evil spirits sent by bad people.

The second lot was some roots of some herbal tree, which every member of the family would put in bath water. They then used that water to wash from top to bottom, rebuking the spirit of witchcraft to leave them. They were not to use soap, and they would have to drip-dry because use of towels was forbidden.

For the third one, they were given two rhino horns with red and black beads. They had to bury these somewhere on the thatch of one of the huts. By applying these, it meant whenever evil spirits visited their home, they would see only a pool of blood, and the home would become invisible.

After all the instructions, Bijou and Bernard paid Toutswe for his service through two bullocks, which were driven to his kraal in the middle of the night seven days later. They followed what he had instructed them to do.

"What then do you make of Toutswe, Bernard?" Bijou asked.

"Well, he knows what he is talking about. If we did not go, we would not have known who our enemies were," Bernard said confidently.

"Yet when you see Sintu and Bayeme, you would not expect them to be against us."

"Well, darling, they don't have to go around with that written on their foreheads," Bernard countered.

"It just goes to show that you can't always tell that a pumpkin has bad seeds inside it! We trusted them so much, and yet people are not always what they seem."

CHAPTER 7

The Chief Is Informed of the Outcome of the Inquest

Chief Muyabwo was forty-five years of age and was a cantankerous man. He was six feet ten inches tall, very dark in complexion, and well built. He had no mercy for any one. Due to him being a heavy drinker, he had the belly the size of a basketball, but strangely enough, women found it attractive because it showed he was a powerful man with a lot of money. Whenever Muyabwo was coming, one could tell from his footsteps, because he was heavy footed. He had big feet, and his shoes were specially made for him. Most of his clothes were made to fit because he could not fit the normal sizes. He had one squinting eye from birth, which made him look menacing.

As advised by Toutswe, the witch doctor, Bijou and Bernard went to report to the chief of their findings regarding the death of Sarah. They got to the chief's place around ten in the morning. The chief was all ready to carry out his daily duties and had nothing scheduled for that particular time.

The chief's private police met them as they entered the gate and asked them their reason for coming to see the chief.

"Our daughter, Sarah, died a few weeks ago and we are coming to report the findings to the chief," Bernard explained.

"The chief has nothing scheduled for this time, if you just wait outside the court room, then I just go and inform him of your arrival," Barry the security man said.

"My Lord I have some villagers coming to report the cause of the death for their daughter Sarah."

"Well, bring them straight in!" chief Muyabwo said with a loud voice.

Barry took them in and got them seated and he also sat down in preparation for the hearing.

"Tell me Bernard, what actually happened?"

"My Lord, as we went to find out from Toutswe what was the cause of Sarah's death, he told us some shocking news." Bernard explained shaking with anger.

"Toutswe viewed the cause of the death through the spirit medium and was shown that Sarah was bewitched," Bernard continued to explain.

"What! I am not going to have witches wasting anybody's life as long as I am still ruling."

"Did he tell you who the witches are?"

"Yes my Lord, he said it was Sintu and Bayeme."

"I suspected the two, Toutswe is right! I have never liked them."

"My Lord, Toutswe is a great witch doctor, as he looked through his mirror he could see a big shadow and two goblins standing by Sarah on the night she died. The goblins even told Sarah that they were not going to leave her alive." Bernard reiterated.

"Well they are going to regret this, as for me, Chief Muyabwo, I believe in tit for tat as a fair game."

"I will give them a death sentence; witches will not last in my village."

"I am going to show everybody who lives around this area that I will not tolerate anybody bewitching anybody else in this village."

"Barry! I want you with immediate effect to go and bring Sintu and Bayeme."

"Togo, bring Toutswe the witch doctor. I want this finished today," the chief said, heating the ground with his stick.

Barry and Togo were his security men. During those days, chiefs were allowed to employ about two security men and three private police. Both Barry and Togo went to carry out the chief's orders. Sintu and Bayeme were busy at home as usual and were shocked when they saw Barry arriving. Methuselah was present, helping his parents as they worked together as a family.

"Is there a problem?" Bayeme asked anxiously.

"The chief wants you and your wife immediately."

"Why are we being summoned? Have we done something wrong to be summoned together?"

"You will soon find out from him. It's not for me to know why he is summoning you. Can we go now? He is waiting."

"Methuselah, continue with what you doing. We will see you soon."

Methuselah said, "Mum, can I come with you?"

"No, you cannot come. We are not aware of why the chief summoned us," Sithu said, trembling.

"I hope we are going to be all right. If not, what will happen to Methuselah?"

"Lord, Lord! Please let nothing happen to us. Methuselah has nobody to look after him." Sithu started sobbing tears.

Sithu and Bayeme were shaking because they could sense something was not right. Sithu was in tears even though she tried not to be seen by Methuselah crying. Bayeme tried to comfort Sithu and said that she had no reason to cry. They had done nothing wrong to the chief or to anybody in the village. Meanwhile, Barry followed them around to make sure they didn't escape.

Eventually they proceeded to the chief's village, walking in front of Barry. Little did they realise that Methuselah was following, going through the bushes to stay out of sight. He was very concerned why the chief had summoned his parents. Methuselah kept hiding where no one could see him. By that time, he was twelve years of age and was protective of his parents.

They arrived at the chief's place. Barry brought them before the chief. As they were brought before the chief, they immediately saw Bijou and Bernard.

"Are you aware of the reason why I called you?" the chief asked.

"No, my Lord," they answered fearfully.

"What happened to Sarah?"

"My Lord, we know nothing about the cause of Sarah's death. We were also concerned about what could have happened," Bayeme answered.

"Why would you ask us what happened to Sarah? How are we supposed to know?" Sithu cried.

"Shut up, Sithu! Your crying will change nothing," the chief said. "You bewitched Sarah didn't you? How could you shorten a child's life like that?

As I have said before, no one will get away with witchcraft in this village. Every villager is going to learn from you that witchcraft is not allowed as long as I am still the chief of this village."

Sithu and Bayeme continued crying and denying the allegations, but the chief would not listen and had no sympathy for them. He had a lot of faith in Toutswe, the witch doctor.

In no time, Togo arrived with Toutswe.

"Toutswe! Could you confirm what the spirit medium revealed to you about Sarah's death?" Chief Muyabwo loudly asked.

"My Lord, the spirit medium revealed that Sarah was bewitched by Sithu and Bayeme. I was even shown what transpired that night when she died. Sithu and Bayeme are very cruel people and showed no sympathy for that kid. I was shown that there was a shadow standing by Sarah that night and two goblins. The goblins told Sarah that they were not going to leave her alive," Toutswe confidently said.

"Well, Toutswe, I am satisfied by your findings and am going to go ahead with my judgement," the chief reiterated. "I am going to give you both a death sentence. Barry and Togo, take them away and kill them mercilessly."

"Please, my Lord! We know nothing about witchcraft! We insist that Toutswe is wrong with those findings."

"Toutswe is a great witch doctor, and his findings are always right. I have dealt with him for so many years, and everything he has found has always been right."

Sithu and Bayeme started crying, begging the chief to release them because Methuselah had no one to look after him. The chief ignored their plight and continued with the death penalty.

When they were being taken away, Methuselah came out from the hiding and started crying for the chief to not have his parents killed. "Please, Chief Muyabwo. Release my mum and dad. When I grow up I will give you anything that you want from me," Methuselah begged.

"Take that kid away immediately! I will not listen to his plea."

Methuselah was taken away, but the men struggled with him because he was a strong boy. He had grown quite tall for his twelve years. The chief's men took him to one of the villagers who was known to be close to his parents. They informed the villager to keep monitoring Methuselah until further notice. The villager asked anxiously why they had brought him but could not get any satisfactory answer.

Methuselah's parents were hanged. As they were dying, they continued to cry about what was going to happen to Methuselah until their last breath. After the last breath, the chief sent his men to call Bayeme's parents, who lived in the next village, to collect the bodies for burial. Togo and Barry went as instructed.

When Bayeme's parents saw the chief's men arriving, they started panicking because they knew it was unusual. "What brings you here?" Bayeme's dad asked. "Is everything okay with Sithu and Bayeme?"

"Unfortunately, the situation is not right with both Bayeme and Sithu."

"What do you mean by that?" Bayeme's dad said strongly. "Don't tell me my son is dead?"

"They are both dead."

"What? Neither of them was ill!" Bayeme's mother said. She threw herself on the ground and started crying.

"How did it happen?"

"They have been hanged because they were accused of bewitching Sarah."

"Oh, my word! But none of them knew anything about witchcraft."

"We are only messengers. The chief wants you to collect the bodies for burial."

"Oh, Lord! We don't deserve this. What are we going to do with Methuselah?" Bayeme's parents cried.

"Only God in heaven will exact revenge. No one can challenge Chief Muyabwo. How can he waste people's lives like that and get away with it all the time? Never mind. We will go see their bodies and make arrangements for their burial. My Lord, life has turned nasty. How can we bury Bayeme when were expecting him to bury us? Why would Chief Muyabwo do this to us?"

They followed the chief's men to view the bodies. When they got there, Bayeme's mother fainted because she could not believe that could happen to her only son and daughter-in-law. They put her under a tree where it was very cool, and after a few minutes, she came around. As soon as she could stand, she looked at the bodies again and could not stop crying.

Bayeme's father, as a man, was fuming but knew there was very little he could do to express his anger. "What a way to go for my son and daughter-in-law. I am horrified by your death, but I am too weak to fight the chief and his men."

They later made some arrangements to carry Sithu and Bayeme to Sarowe's village. At the same time, they sent someone to let Sithu's family know about the deaths. Sithu's family could not believe it when they heard the news, and then they saw the bodies. Bayeme's and Sithu's families were torn to pieces and could not understand what the world had come to. It was so difficult to know how they could handle Methuselah because he could not stop crying. He felt as if the whole world had come to an end. He had been so close to his parents. Methuselah touched everyone who was at the funeral, and he kept crying for God to take him so he could be with his parents.

The whole village was shaken by the news. Methuselah was broken-hearted, and no one could control him. At twelve years old, he was so close to his parents, and he felt very bitter about losing them. Arrangements were made to bury Sithu and Bayeme, and they were laid to rest two days after they had been hanged. The chief and his family, as well as Bijou and Bernard, did not attend the funeral.

A week after the funeral, when all the mourners had dispensed, Methuselah's grandparents had a meeting to see what was best for him. It was agreed that it would be better for him to stay with his dad's parents because the school was a short distance from them. Bayeme's parents lived in the village next to Sarowe.

The news spread around the village and the surrounding villages. Most people knew Sithu and Bayeme and were not happy about the chief's judgement. Whenever people met, they would discuss what had happened with their neighbours. Most villagers could not understand how human beings, in their normal senses, could come to such a decision.

"What do you think about what happened to Sithu and Bayeme?" Pat, one of the villagers, asked another person.

"Well, what a way to go, particularly for Sithu and Bayeme," Teki commented.

"I only hope one day Chief Muyabwo will get it all back to him. He has been a tyrant for a long time, and it seems there is no end to it."

"Methuselah is now an orphan for no good reason. Could there be anything worse than that?"

"Time will tell. As they say, you reap what you sow. It will all come back to him at some point."

After the lengthy discussion, Pat and Teki departed and continued with what they were doing. For some time, there were tensions in the village because most of them got on very well with Sithu and Bayeme. The main concern was that the allegations made against the deceased were unjustified.

CHAPTER 8

The Struggle to Cope as an Orphan

Every morning as Methuselah got up to go to school, he felt as though his parents were still there for him. He cried his heart out daily when he thought about how he was going to manage without them.

"Grandma, how could I be so unfortunate to lose both my parents just like that? Mum and Dad did not deserve such a death," Methuselah said.

"Life is so difficult, my dear. We are so disturbed about their death. Every day, we are battling to live with this," Grandma replied. She cuddled him and tried to console him. She knew she could never find appropriate words to say to him.

On the other hand, Granddad was going through the worst time of his life. As a man, he was contemplating revenge, but how could that happen? Chief Muyabwo was a powerful man.

At school, Methuselah did not find it any easier. Other kids left him out on the grounds that his parents had been hanged because of witchcraft. The teachers tried their best to support him, but words failed them regarding what to say to him. Other kids were scared of him and made horrible remarks about witches. There could not have been a worse time for a child of twelve, when he needed so much love and care.

It appeared that Methuselah was very lonely at school. No one wanted to be friends with him after what happened. That started affecting his performance at school, and the teachers invited his grandparents to discuss how he could be helped. They agreed that Methuselah was better off living in a different environment. The decision was made to send Methuselah to Biet Bridge, where Sithu's parents lived.

Bayeme's parents continued to talk about their loss and were very concerned about their grandson. One evening they sat down with Methuselah and filled him in about the move to Biet Bridge. They made sure he understood the reason behind the move. They had to be very careful about how to break the news of moving him without hurting him. Methuselah agreed to the move and was happy to leave the village school because he was too much of a loner.

The following weekend after the meeting with the teachers, his grandparents packed all his clothes and whatever he required. Early Saturday morning, they caught the bus going to Biet Bridge. Methuselah was quiet on the way, and they did not know whether he was happy to move.

"Methuselah, why are you so quiet? Don't you want to move?" Grandma asked.

"Grandma, I have lost all my happiness. I thought the world of my mum and dad. They loved me so much and would do anything for me," Methuselah said. "I think it is for the best that I move from the village next to Sarowe and change schools. I am sure God is with me, and he will send his angels to look after me." Methuselah continued to shed tears. "But one thing for sure: I am going to take revenge. Time will tell."

"How? My grandson, please keep away from that ruthless man. I don't want to lose you as well," his grandmother replied.

His granddad felt bad because he thought as a man, he should have done something to get revenge.

When they arrived at his mother's homeland, Sithu's mother met them at the entrance. She welcomed Methuselah and gave him a big hug, but she could not help crying. "Thank you for bringing him to me. At least my mind is at rest seeing him every day," Sithu's mother remarked.

After greeting one another, they went on to discuss their loss. Both grandmothers hoped that God would give them strength to look after their grandson. They agreed that the decision to move Methuselah was a good idea. Certainly the new environment would do him some good. Meanwhile, Methuselah sat and listened to all that was discussed.

Sithu's and Bayeme's parents spent a couple days together in Biet Bridge consoling one another. Methuselah was spoiled with both his grandparents together. After two days, the Bayeme's parents decided to go back, and they gave their grandson a bit of pocket money. They also stressed the point that they would always be there for Methuselah when he needed them. It seemed they were quite happy for Methuselah to stay with his other grandparents in a new environment.

After a few weeks in Biet Bridge, it seemed Methuselah liked it there. His grandparents made a lot of fuss over him and disliked to see him unhappy. Also, Aunt Violet and her family often took him to their home and gave all the support he required, as did Uncle Denise and his family.

The other reason Methuselah liked living with his mother's parents was that as soon as he started living with them, they found him a lovely Alsatian dog, which was very adorable. It was a white male dog named Rees. Rees appeared to be Methuselah's best friend and followed him everywhere. He would play with Methuselah as if he was playing with another dog.

In the morning, Methuselah did not need an alarm clock. Rees would start barking outside his door at 6 a.m. As soon as Rees started barking, Methuselah would know it was time to take him for a walk. Rees used to get so excited as soon as he saw Methuselah coming out of his bedroom. He would jump all over him, barking and wagging his tail. Methuselah would give him a cuddle and a kiss before taking him for a walk. Rees meant a lot to him because he could chat to him as if he was chatting to a human being.

Within a short space of time, Aunt Violet found a school that was convenient for Methuselah. He started attending school at Pumula Primary School. He soon settled and liked it better than Bait Primary School in Sarowe village. As before, Methuselah was always committed to his schoolwork and never gave his grandparents any hassle regarding homework. He made new friends and was liked by many children in his class because he was very bright. His friends were named Mob, Ricky, and Ben. All his friends and classmates thought the world of him.

Life seemed to have taken another turn for Methuselah compared to when he had been living with his other grandparents after his parents' deaths. After he moved to Biet Bridge, it seemed he could mix well with other children. All children around him accepted him. He still missed his parents but seemed to have accepted that he had to learn to live with his loss.

Methuselah had always helped his parents, and he continued to help his grandparents. He assisted them around the home, in the garden, and in the fields. His grandparents were surprised that a child of his age could work so hard.

"Methuselah, my grandson, you were well trained," his grandmother said.

"I have been trained to do everything, I can even do my own ironing," Methuselah informed his grandma. "My mum and dad were hard workers, and they trained me to be the same. I am happy that they did, because now they are no more. What would happen if I had to depend on them for everything? I like to help where I can."

Grandma was touched by the way he spoke, and she went in her bedroom and started crying. She quickly pulled herself together again and went back to Methuselah because she did not want him to see her crying. "Methuselah, let's go to the back garden and get you some fruit, if you are interested in raspberries and some gooseberries," she said.

"Yes, Grandma, I love them."

They took a plate and went to the back garden. All the fruits were quite ripe. They enjoyed eating the fruit and later went inside the house to relax. As evening drew near, Grandma started cooking the evening meal.

Meanwhile, Granddad and Methuselah made sure that all the cattle were in the kraal and then closed the gate. He made sure that the cattle were well secured and that they would not come out; that would mean they would destroy their neighbour's crops in the fields.

In the evening, as they relaxed after an evening meal, Grandma asked her grandson how he was getting on at school. He indicated that he was much happier at Pumula Primary School than when he'd been at Bait School. He said at Pumula, most of the kids were friendly.

"At the other school, I was very lonely and isolated after Mum and Dad's death. At Pumula, I am getting on with everybody."

Grandma and Granddad were more than happy to know that he was well settled at school. At that stage, they couldn't have wished for anything better than to know their grandson was comfortable and got on well with the other children.

"Well, darling, Grandma and Granddad are going to have some tea before we go to bed. What about you? Would you like some?" Grandma asked.

"No, Grandma. I don't have tea at night because I am afraid I might go in a deep sleep and wet the bed," he said, laughing.

After that, they decided to go to bed. Before that, Grandma took him to the toilet. They used a pit toilet, which was built a few yards from the house. A pit toilet needed to be a bit farther from the main house because it was quite smelly. They were very ancient toilets, which were very different from modern toilets, because they could not be flushed. Also, in rural areas using a toilet at night would mean taking some risks: because it was dark, one would never know who would be knocking about. At the same time, because it was dark, snakes could be crawling. Snakes in Africa were very dangerous; one could end up dying from a bite because many snakes were poisonous.

Grandma told her grandson that they were lucky they had a toilet, because without one they would be stuck. She said one night, an old lady who lived in the village went outside behind her mud hut to pass urine, and it was very dark. Suddenly, someone came and hit her on her buttocks, and the old lady rushed back in the house before she'd finished passing urine. She said she ended up wetting herself. From that time onwards, the old lady could not tell who'd hit her. The lady had no toilet, and from that day onwards she was so scared of going out at night to pass urine. Methuselah found that very funny, and he could not stop laughing. After that story, they both retired and went to sleep.

CHAPTER 9

Back in Sarowe Village, Bijou and Bernard Were Dejected

Three months after Sithu and Bayeme's deaths, Sarah's parents struggled to cope with life. Villagers and other neighbouring people could not get over the hanging of Sithu and Bayeme. Bijou and Bernard found life difficult because most villagers blamed them for what had happened. As they talked about the episode, one could tell how distressed they were getting.

"Bernard, life seems to be hard going in this village, I know we lost Sarah, but how are we going to live with the hanging of Sithu and Bayeme?"

"Bijou, life is complicated. What could we have done to avoid this from happening? We are hurt by the death of Sarah."

"We might have to move from this village because we have become very unpopular with everyone."

"What? Don't talk rubbish! What do you mean, move? We have all the backing of the chief. Who cares whether we become popular or not? Sod the villagers. Chief Muyabwo is on our side, and that's what matters.

"But we are not living in a vacuum, where we won't worry about other people," Bijou stressed. "One of these fine days, I will run away if the situation remains as it is."

"Well, Bijou, it's entirely up to you what you want to do, but I am not moving anywhere—and neither are the kids. Is that clear? I was born here and will reside here all my life. That's too bad for anyone who dislikes me."

"You know what? Sometimes I struggle to understand you, Bernard. You seem to be in your own world, don't you? In life you need other people. Life loses meaning when everybody seems to be against you."

"Listen, Bijou. That's enough of that. We cannot live to please people at the expense of our children. Sarah died mysteriously, and I am not going to budge on that. Someone had to face the consequences. I don't care how."

As Bernard got upset about the whole issue, Bijou knew it was time to keep quiet. Bernard had to walk away for the argument to not get out of hand. As a man, he did not want to show his wife Bijou that things were not right. Bijou knew deep down that she was not happy living in the village. It seemed the good old days had gone, and life had become unbearable. Though the chief was on their side, she needed company from other villagers. She made up her mind that if life continued to be difficult in the village, she would move away. Bijou went to a secret place and started sobbing tears about what had happened in their lives. She thought her husband was being hard on her, and he did not seem to understand what she was going through with the villagers.

As the situation worsened in the village, Bijou and Bernard's lives continued to be miserable. Bijou went to seek advice from her friends because she could not cope anymore. Her friends advised her to be strong, and the situation would eventually improve. On the other hand, Bernard did not see the need to move because he thought he would be able to handle the situation.

Meanwhile, life became more difficult because the other children were also missing Sarah.

"Mum, if Sarah was here, she would be helping you with housework," Tina said.

"I know, Tina! Life has not been the same since Sarah died."

"I wish she was still alive," said Leonard, Sarah's only brother.

The kids continued to talk about Sarah. For Bijou, it was as though someone was reopening a wound that was trying to heal. All she prayed for was for God to give her strength because she felt she was going to break down. She continued to put on a brave face for the children.

With time, she decided to visit her parents in Gaberone, which was thirty miles from Sarowe village. She felt she had gone through a lot and wanted a break from the village. Bijou decided to leave the village without telling anyone. She tried to leave at night but was caught by Tina her daughter.

"Mum, what are you doing? You've got all your bags packed. Why?" Tina asked.

"Shush! I don't want anyone to know, not even your dad. I am going to see Grandma and Granddad."

"What about Leonard and me? What are we going to do?" Tina asked.

"Dad will look after you," Mum reassured her. "Please promise, Tina, that you won't tell anyone about my going away. I have had enough, and I feel I need a break."

"Okay, Mum. I promise I won't tell anyone, not even Dad," Tina reassured her.

"I will be back in two weeks' time. I just need a break from this village. Please look after Leonard. I love you both. I will see you when I see you. God bless."

Bijou gave Tina a hug and told her to go to bed.

Then Bijou took her bags and went away. It was quite dark outside, but Bijou didn't care what might happen to her. She walked until she could find transport. As she walked along the road to Gaberone, she saw a car coming and stopped it.

"What are you doing at this time of the night, woman?" the man driving the van asked.

"I need a lift to Gaberone, please!"

"You have to be careful. You are putting your life at risk."

"I have gone through a lot in my life and could not care less what happens to me."

Bijou was given a lift to her parents' house in Gaberone. At that time, it was about two in the morning, and her parents had gone to sleep. She knocked on their bedroom window. They woke up panicking because they were not expecting her.

"What's going on, Bijou? Why are you travelling at this time of the morning?"

"Mum, I will tell you about it later. Just let me go to sleep."

"What about something to eat?"

"No, Mum, I don't need anything to eat at this time, thank you. All I want is just to go to sleep."

"Okay, Bijou. Speak to you later."

"Sleep well."

In the morning, Bijou explained to her parents the reason why she had come home. She made them aware that from the time Sarah had died, things hadn't been very good in Sarowe. What had made the situation worse was the hanging of Sithu and Bayeme.

"Mum, as I am still grieving, the villagers have made it difficult for me and my children. I feel like a traitor. Yes, Sithu and Bayeme were hanged due to some allegations made against them regarding bewitching Sarah, but that was the chief's decision, not ours. Villagers have taken it upon themselves to treat my family badly. I feel excluded. I feel humiliated, and I have lost respect from every villager." She started crying.

"Please don't cry. We understand very well what you are going through, but we want you to be strong for the benefit of the children," her mother said.

"What's making it worse is that it's straining my relationship with Bernard. I have been trying to talk to him to make him see sense. Mum and Dad, I want you to do me a favour: don't let anyone know that I am here, not even Bernard."

"But how can we hide that from your own husband? We get on very well with Bernard and we are unhappy about hiding anything from him."

"Mum, please do as I am telling you. All I want is just a complete break from everything."

That morning, Bernard at the village discovered that Bijou was missing. He searched everywhere for his wife to no avail. He rowed with Tina, whom he believed knew where her mother was.

"Tina, where is your mother? I am sure you know where she is."

"Dad, I have no clue of her whereabouts."

"Please don't do this to me Tina," her dad insisted. "How can Bijou do this to me when we are already going through a lot in our life?"

He continued with his search but did not get anywhere. He immediately went to see the chief with regards to the care of the children. The chief and his senior wife had no objection to that. He then left the children with the chief and his senior wife in order to go look for Bijou in Gaberone. At that point, he did not mind what time of the day it was, all he wanted was to find his wife. He managed to find transport to Gaberone quite easily, and off he went.

As he got to Bijou's parents' home, he greeted them as usual. Before long he told them he was looking for Bijou.

"What do you mean, where is she?" his mother-in-law asked.

Bernard raised his voice. "Please don't play games with me! If she is not here, where would she be?"

"Well, that's news to us, Bernard. We are not even aware that she has gone missing. I hope she is OK, wherever she is."

Meanwhile Bijou had gone into hiding, she was living with her cousin, who lived ten kilometres from her parents' home.

Bernard searched everywhere for Bijou in vain. He started interrogating Bijou's parents, demanding them to tell him where she was. Her parents insisted that they did not know where she had gone. Bernard seemed to be running out of time, and so he decided to alert the police because he was getting concerned about her safety. He went to the nearest police station to file a report.

As he walked in, the senior police attended to him. "Yes, sir, how can we help?"

"My wife has gone missing, and I have no clue where I can find her."

"How long has she been missing?"

"At least three days, sir."

"Three days? Why didn't you report this straightaway?"

"I thought she had visited her parents, but it was a wrong assumption."

The police requested some more details from him that could help with their search. Bernard gave them all the information as per their request. As he left the police station, he felt so fed up and wondered whether he would ever find her. He went back to inform Bijou's parents that he had filled a report to the police. After that, he decided to go back to Sarowe to make sure the children were OK.

When he got home, the children were anxious to know whether he'd managed to find their mother. Further, Chief Muyabwo and his wife were also waiting to hear the news. It seemed the children had been under good care because they did not make any complaints. Bernard accepted that he had to wait for the police's findings, and he continued to take care of the children on his own.

After two weeks, Bijou felt she had had a good break. She informed her parents of her intention to go back to Sarowe village because she missed her husband and children. Her parents agreed to the decision because they were also worried about the two children. She set off on a Sunday afternoon, waited for transport, and eventually got a bus, which only took thirty minutes to get to the village.

As she approached her gate, she could see villagers staring at her without saying anything to her. She could sense she was unwelcome amongst the villagers, but she thought she would not take any notice of them. She wanted to be with her children and her husband.

The children were very happy to see her. They gave her a hug and told her how much they had missed her. On the other hand, her husband was a bit subdued. He was troubled by the fact that she could have left him and the children without saying where she was going.

"What is the problem, Bernard? You are not yourself."

"The problem is I have been very worried about you. How can you do this to me and the children? Where have you been, darling? I looked everywhere for you, including your parents' place. That was unreasonable. You could have at least said where you were going."

"I do apologize, but I just felt I wanted a break. Otherwise I was going to break down."

"I know, love. But that was not the best way to go about it."

"Aren't you excited to see me back?"

"Of course I am, Bijou." He smiled and gave her a big hug.

"How are things here, Bernard?"

"It will take long for the dust to settle. I wouldn't worry so much about the villagers."

"We will pull through. Together, we are strong."

After that, Bijou spent more time with the children, asking them how they had been getting on at school and at home since she had been away. Then she went around the home to make sure everything was still intact. In a way, she was glad to be back with her family because it was not easy to separate from them for such a length of time.

CHAPTER 10

Character Changing

Time passed, and grieving Methuselah's mood deteriorated. Most times he would try to put on a brave face, but deep down life was not easy for him. He continued changing in character because there was nothing that could make things any easier. The amount of stress he was going through was too much for a child of his age, but he tried hard to be as brave as a lion. As a human being, he could not hide his grief any longer, and he started being unpleasant and aggressive towards other children. He was withdrawn all the time at school and was generally unhappy. He lost interest even in his best friends. All he wanted was to be left alone.

"Methuselah, do you want to play football after school today?" his friend Mob asked.

"No, at present I would rather be left alone."

"But we have been great friends since you came to this school," said Ben, another good friend.

"Well, times are changing, and I don't need friends anymore."

"We could still make you happy, as we have always done," Ricky said.

"Please, guys, do me a favour and leave me alone. I will play with you whenever I feel like it, OK?"

With those words, they left Methuselah alone. They could not understand what was going on with him. They went home and told their parents how Methuselah had changed and had lost any interest in his friends.

The teachers noticed his unbecoming behaviour and tried to see how best they could help him. Each time they called him in the office to try to talk to him, he would not show any interest. Other children reported him being rude and aggressive towards them. He was completely out of character.

His grandparents also noticed the change in him but were in denial. They tried to talk to him, but all he said was he missed his parents, and then he would burst into tears. His grandparents were heartbroken as he continued to feel that way.

"Methuselah, you know we don't want to see you in that state. We want you to be happy," his grandparents said.

"I am never going to be the same," Methuselah said. "I was with my parents, laughing and joking, the day when they were hanged! How can that ever come out of my brain? To be honest with you, Grandma, I am struggling to live with this. I am hoping that one day this suffering will be all over."

"Please don't talk like that. You are breaking my heart, Methuselah. You know I love you very much, and I want to give you the support you need."

"Yes, I am aware of that. But the children I know have their parents, and I am the only orphan at school. Grandma, I know life is not easy. I know you are kind to me. But being an orphan is the worst situation in anyone's life. I know it's now two years since I lost my parents, but I will never get over it." He burst into tears again.

His grandparents were deeply saddened and did not know how to make him feel any better. They continued to help him in the best way they could. At school the teachers were still not sure of what was going on. They invited his grandparents to discuss the situation and how best they could help him. After the meeting with his grandparents, the teachers understood why his behaviour had changed. Methuselah was not involved in the meeting as per his grandparents' request; they did not want him to break down.

Methuselah decided that it was the best to leave school because he felt unable to concentrate. He battled to live with his loss for a while, and eventually he fell into a depression. His grandparents, aunt, and uncle tried their best to show how much they loved and cared for him, but it was all in vain. He went through phases in which he would self-harm.

One day his grandmother saw him with cuts all over his hands. Highly disturbed, she exclaimed, "Methuselah, what has happened to your hands? You have cuts all over!"

"That's how life goes. I appreciate all your concern, but the parental love is missing in my life. I love you all very much, but I hope you understand how I feel."

"But, Methuselah! I need to know what has happened. How did you get those cuts?"

"Don't worry about it. I am fine."

His grandmother could not figure out what had happened, but she did not want to keep asking him further questions. She explained to him how much he meant to them and said that they were not happy to see him in that state. She said they would do anything to make him feel better.

"Grandma, you are doing all you can to make me feel better, and I appreciate it very much. But with what I have gone through, I am very difficult to please."

Later, Grandma discussed with her husband how best they could try to help their grandchild. It seemed they did not know how best to handle the situation. The following day, they called their son and daughter to find out if they could come up with a solution. They decided to continue giving him all the support he needed and to keep monitoring him all the time. Up to that time, they were still not sure of how he'd gotten the cuts on both hands, and he would not tell anyone how it had happened.

Methuselah started getting sleepless nights, and when he did manage to sleep, he would suffer from nightmares. One night as he was sleeping, he dreamt he was chatting to his mum and dad, and it seemed so real. He told them how much he missed them, and he wished he could reverse the clock. He felt the warmth of them being around and laughing and joking as if they were alive. As the dream ended, he felt they had gone, and he begged for them to stay. "Mum and Dad, please stay! I so very much need you in my life."

As he finished saying that, he woke up and found his grandma and granddad standing by him. They had been woken up by him calling out in his sleep.

"What's the matter, son?"

"Grandma, I dreamt my mum and dad were chatting to me as if they were alive."

"Oh, dear. What a dream! It's all in your mind, son. Probably Mum and Dad are not very happy. They might be worrying about you. I think you'd better come sleep with us, love. You might sleep better."

"OK, Grandma. I will do as you say."

That night he had a better night. It appeared he was feeling insecure about sleeping on his own. His grandparents felt the same for him and continually shared the same bed with him for a while.

Though his grandparents were quite supportive, they were quite concerned about him. They loved him dearly but could not fill the gap of missing his parents. They did all they could to help him grow in a good environment where everybody around him cared a lot about him.

In the daytime, Methuselah would spend more time with Rees, his dog. He made sure Rees had been fed and gave him all the love he needed. They would go for long walks together, during which Methuselah would chat to him.

"Rees, if it was not for you, I would be very lonely. I feel you are loyal to me. You are the best thing that has happened to me since my parents died. I only wish you were a human being so I could tell you how I feel inside."

With time, he started sneaking Rees into his bedroom. He felt insecure and did not want to keep sharing the same bedroom with his grandparents. His dog continued to sleep in his room for a while before his grandparents noticed. Normally in Africa, dogs slept outside.

One night Rees was desperate for a wee, and he started barking while standing by the door. Methuselah woke up and knew he had to take him out to relieve himself. "OK, Rees. I know you want to wee. Come on, then." He opened the door and took him outside.

Immediately his grandparents opened the door to see what was going on because they'd heard Rees barking in Methuselah's room. "What's going on, Methuselah? Is Rees sleeping in your bedroom?" Granddad said.

"Yes, Granddad. I felt secure with him sleeping in my room."

"You have to be careful, because you don't want to be taking him out on your own at this time of the night. You don't know who is knocking about."

"Okay, Granddad. Tomorrow I will take him for a short walk before I go to sleep."

Then Methuselah asked Granddad whether he had any objections to Rees sleeping in his room. Granddad said he did not mind. His concern was simply that it was unsafe when Methuselah had to take Rees out for a wee at that time of the night. They both went back into their rooms and slept.

CHAPTER 11

Suicide Attempt

Methuselah, now sixteen, was getting more depressed. The emptiness of missing his parents relentlessly attacked him. Life had lost its meaning for him. Each day was a struggle to live. Eventually he felt he could not take any more.

One evening he decided to take a walk to contemplate what he could do to end his suffering. As he went through the thick forests, he walked along the River Muyanezi. It was quite deep, and there was always so much water in the river at any time of the year. There were rumours of people having seen crocodiles in that river. Villagers were conscious not to let their children go anywhere near the river.

As Methuselah walked along the river, he felt it would be better to end his life somewhere where nobody would ever see him again. Deep down he knew that his grandparents thought the world of him, but at the same time he knew that no one could ever take the place of his parents.

Rees was following him along the river. Methuselah tried to send him back home, but Rees kept reappearing. Methuselah felt guilty about what would happen to Rees when he had taken his life, but he tried to put that to the back of his mind. He stood and talked to the dog for a while. He told him how much he loved him and how much he would miss him, but Methuselah said he had no choice. Rees began to cry loud as if to stop him from what he was going to do.

He cuddled Rees for a while and shed a few tears, but like a warrior, he had to carry out his mission regardless of how much he thought of his dog. After, that he pursued his intentions. "If I end my life in this river, nobody will ever find me. Crocodiles will devour me, and that will be the end of my suffering," Methuselah said to himself.

He continued along the river and came across a cliff. As he stood on top, ready to throw himself into the river, he heard a voice.

"Methuselah! Methuselah, stop! I know what you are going through, but stop and listen to what I am going to say."

"Who is speaking? Please come out in the open. The voice seems familiar, but I can't see you."

"I am your father! Methuselah, please! Do not take your life. I want you to live longer because there are so many good things ahead of you."

"Where are you, Father? I can only hear your voice. I cannot see you. Please let me see your face. Perhaps that could put my mind at rest."

"No, no! The dead and the living don't mix," the voice continued.

"I am troubled, Father. Since the day you died, life has lost its meaning, I have searched for peace of mind but have failed."

"What you must realise is that you are now a man, my son, and taking your life is a sign of weakness. Stand like a man and fight like a man. I want you one day to take revenge! Revenge, revenge! Fear not, for I will be with you through the whole fight. I will pray to the Almighty to open up the ways of how you can do it. I am behind you in everything you do. Seek Revenge!" The voice faded.

"Father, your voice is gone! Please stay and keep talking to me! It has been great talking to you; it seemed as though you had come back to life. Yes, I will get revenge as you have said, no matter what it takes and no matter how long it takes me to do so."

Methuselah said to himself, "The voice was definitely my father's voice. I need to carry on the mission as assigned."

He listened to the voice and took the mission seriously. He decided to go back home, but this time he was content and felt strongly that he could face life as it was. What the voice said rang continuously in his ears for a while. As he descended the cliff, Rees suddenly appeared, and Methuselah wondered where the dog had been hiding whilst he was standing on top of the cliff.

"Let's go home, Rees. What a wonderful dog you are. I am proud of you. Don't worry—I will not try to take my life again," Methuselah reassured him.

At home, his grandparents had noticed he had been gone for a while and had been wondering where he was. As soon as they saw him, they felt relieved.

"Where have you been, son? We were getting worried," Grandma asked.

"I went for a walk with Rees down the river."

"What? At this time of the night? Well, young man, don't take such risks. People have seen crocodiles in that river. Are you aware of that?"

"Don't worry, Grandma. I am back now. I do apologize if I got you worried. I shan't go there again at this time of the night."

Time passed, and since hearing the voice, Methuselah appeared more focused with life. He started making plans for the future, planning to look for a job because that was a way forward to be able to carry out the mission. After the day he'd heard the voice, his grandparents could see a change in him. It seemed he had learnt to stand like a man in life.

Methuselah moved on despite his loss. What his father told him about revenging remained a secret. All he kept thinking about was how to take revenge. It was his secret, and he was not going to reveal it to anyone else. Certainly he knew time would tell how he would carry it out.

CHAPTER 12

Methuselah Gets a Job

On a Sunday afternoon, as Methuselah and his grandparents were finishing their lunch, he told them of his intention to go to the Botswana border to look for a job. He said he was a man and felt it was time to stand on his own two feet. He thanked them for looking after him all that time, but he felt it was time that he should move on in life. After a lengthy discussion about what he would do for accommodation, they agreed that for the first few weeks, he would be coming back home until he secured his own accommodation.

On Monday morning, Methuselah got ready to go to the Botswana border, and he bade farewell to his grandparents. They gave him some money for transport. He boarded the bus, which took him directly to his destination. As soon as he arrived, he went to the part of the Botswana border where his father used to work. He saw the senior foreman's office and knocked on his door. As soon as he entered, the foreman asked what his name was.

"Methuselah Tyke."

"Your name rings a bell. Were you related to the late Bayeme Tyke?" asked the senior foreman.

"That was my father, sir. Did you know him?"

"I used to work with him. I am sorry about the way he died."

"Unfortunately, life is very unfair, and there is very little one can do about it."

"Anyway, young man, what can I do for you today?" asked the senior foreman.

"I am looking for a job, if there are any vacancies."

"What sort of job are you looking for?"

"Whatever you can offer. I have no experience or skill."

"I can offer you a security job, if you are an honest man."

"I am sure I can do that, sir. I am more than willing to learn."

"You came just in time. Someone recently retired, and I have not yet filled that vacancy. I will take you, and you will be trained for the job."

"Thank you, sir. I am very grateful."

They sat down and discussed the wages that he was going to be paid weekly. Methuselah was entitled to four weeks' annual leave. He was informed of a probationary period of six weeks, to prove that he was capable of the job. Further, he was advised that punctuality was very important, as was avoiding absenteeism at any other time. The foreman informed him that accommodation was provided because workers would be expected to work shift work, as well as being on call. Methuselah was told to go back home, and he would be expected to start work the following morning.

Filled with excitement, he left the foreman's office, went back to the bus station, and boarded a bus to his grandparents place to collect his clothes. He got there in the early part of the evening and shared his good news. His grandparents were as happy that he did not struggle to find a job. Further, they appreciated that accommodation would be provided.

"Methuselah, I am proud of you! You seem to be more focused with your life now than before," Granddad said.

"A man has to grow at some point and move on with life, despite what they are going through."

"That is the way forward, son. You will not go wrong when you look at life that way. Keep up the good work, and God will bless you with whatever you lack in your life," Grandma reassured him.

Later in the evening, his grandmother assisted him with packing his clothes. They all had an early night because Methuselah had to catch the early bus back to the Botswana border in the morning. Methuselah had a restless night, and he was too excited about his good news. He woke up quite early and got ready to go. He said goodbye to his grandparents and Rees. He told his grandparents he was going to miss them, as well as his best friend, Rees. He told them that as soon as he was settled, he would take Rees with him.

He arrived at work on time and was shown where to put his suitcase. The room was small, with one bed and a space with a few nails on the wall to hang his clothes. There were two blankets and a pillow provided. He was also shown a small kitchen, which was shared. Basic meals were provided, but they had to take turns to prepare them. Later, he was introduced to some of his workmates and then shown what to do.

After some training, he settled into the job well and gained confidence in his everyday tasks. He worked hard all the time and was liked by his superiors. He made friends at work, and one was named Leslie. He also made friends outside of work and even met a nice woman named Kim, to whom he became close. Life began to have meaning because he could tell the woman liked him. The woman worked at the Zimbabwe border as a security officer.

It made such a great difference in his life to know he could work and earn a bit of money for himself. He found that independence was what had been lacking in his life. He managed to get what suited him, and he could go out and enjoy himself, meeting new people in the process. He visited both sets of grandparents several times and told them how he was getting on. Getting a job was the best thing that had ever happened in his life, and he made sure he worked to the best of his ability.

His grandparents were proud of him and continued to support him morally and socially at all times. They made an effort to visit him at his workplace and were very encouraged by what his bosses said about his hard work.

Methuselah certainly made an impression at work, and before long he was promoted to a senior security attendant. Everyone who knew him thought he did well to rise up within a short time. Many people talked about his progress, agreeing that because he was a hard worker, he deserved the promotion. He started earning decent money and bought a stand to build himself his own home near his workplace. Once he had bought this, he went ahead and found some builders to build his home. With material and a plan, in no time he had finished building the bungalow. It had two bedrooms, a large kitchen, a lounge, and a bathroom and toilet together.

Owning a home of his own was quite an achievement on his part. Methuselah felt good for having accomplished such a project. His grandparents visited to look at the bungalow after it was finished and were very happy for him.

"We are proud of you, Methuselah, for owning a place you can call your own. Certainly you have shown that you are mature and able to run your own life without any guidance from anybody," one of his grandmothers said.

In the evening, both sets of grandparents called it a day and went back to their homes. Methuselah took them to the station where they could catch a bus. One thing was for sure: his grandparents were quite close and tried their best to be there for their grandson. Though he was working and living on his own, they still treated him like their baby.

Before long, Methuselah went to his grandparents in Beit Bridge to collect Rees, his dog. Rees was quite pleased to live with Methuselah again. When Methuselah had moved away, Rees would look all around the home, wondering what had happened.

"Welcome, Rees. I did miss you a lot. Thank God I have managed to build my own home, which is big enough to accommodate you. I told you I would take you to live with me as soon as I was settled. It's good to have you back with me, Rees. You are my best friend! You know that, don't you? You have always been there for me when I most needed somebody."

Rees began jumping all over him as if to thank Methuselah for what he had done. Methuselah cuddled him and gave him a kiss. Rees appeared to be quite at home with Methuselah. Before he went to work, Methuselah always made sure Rees had been fed. He also managed to build a nice kennel for the dog. Whenever he came back from work, he would take Rees for long walks to keep him fit. He got a garden where Rees could jump around and wee whenever he wanted to. By that time, Rees was about six years old, but he was still healthy.

CHAPTER 13

Methuselah Invites Kim Out

On a Saturday afternoon, as Methuselah was walking around the town of Gaberone doing a bit of shopping, he saw Kim, the woman he had met before. Kim was eighteen years old, reasonably tall, and slim. She had brown eyes and was angelic looking. She had what a man would look for in a woman. Her hair was long and black, and she had dimples on her cheeks. When she smiled, her teeth were as white as snow. Sooner or later, he had to say something before she questioned why he was staring at her.

"Hey, good to see you."

"Methuselah, how are you doing?"

"Fine, love. What a small world! Have you got time to talk?"

"Yes, I can spare a few minutes. I am not in a great rush."

"Fantastic! I have always wanted to invite you out. I hope you don't mind me using this opportunity."

"Not at all. Go ahead and say what you have to say."

"Thank you, Kim. Is it possible to take you out for a drink, please? If it's okay, which day suits you best?"

"Weekends would be the best time for me. I work full-time during the week. We could go out on a Saturday, like today."

"Oh, great! I am also off most weekends. Will it be okay to meet next Saturday?"

"I am not doing anything next Saturday, so that will be fine."

"Fabulous! I look forward to being seen walking with a beautiful lady like you."

"Thank you, Methuselah."

"Is it okay to meet by the river at 2 p.m., near the Apes?"

"That will be fine with me, Methuselah."

"I am sorry it is such short notice, but I appreciate you accepting the invitation."

The Apes was a beautiful building by the river where lovers would meet and enjoy the quiet, peaceful atmosphere. Methuselah and Kim looked forward to meeting at the river. They parted ways after confirming the date, time, and place to meet. Methuselah was very excited and could not believe that his life was changing in all aspects.

Kim also felt good to be invited out by Methuselah, because he was quite tall and handsome. She went home and told her mother about her date. Her mother was happy for her.

Methuselah went back to his home full of excitement. He looked back on his life and started talking to himself, scolding himself for nearly taking his own life. "One time I felt as if life was coming to an end, but no there is more to life than I imagined. Thank God that I can still look at life positively. Not long ago, I was going to take my own life. If it was not for my father's voice, I would have done it. Certainly God has a good plan for me, and I am very grateful."

That night it took him a long time to get to sleep because he reflected on his past experiences that could have ended his life. Eventually he went to sleep. He had to go to church in the morning, because it was Sunday. When he was in church, he felt he had to say something to testify about his past; maybe someone would benefit from his experiences. He decided to go forward to testify, and most church members were quite touched by his testimony. In fact, when he had finished testifying, some members thanked him for such a strong testimony. Other members told him that they felt quite emotional while he gave his testimony. He did not disclose his plan for revenge because he decided that was something he had to keep a secret.

When church was over, Methuselah went home, prepared some food, and got his clothes ready for work for the following morning. Everything seemed as normal as it could be from the time he'd started. He looked forward to going to work and attending social events.

The week could not go quick enough. Methuselah was looking forward to his date. As Saturday approached he got his best clothes out and spent more time ironing them to make a good impression. He felt he was approaching the best times of his life, and he was going to try to take some steps forward in terms of getting a soul mate.

While talking to one of his friends before the date, Methuselah expressed some concerns. "Leslie, you know I have never had a date before. What am I supposed to do?"

"Oh, my word. What a twit you are," Leslie said, laughing.

"Leslie, this is not a laughing matter. I am serious! For your information, I don't even know how to kiss a woman."

"Don't worry, Methuselah. I will give you a few lessons before you get that far," Leslie reassured him.

His friend realised that Methuselah had been living in a rural environment and was quite unused to being with women from an urban setup. Leslie explained to Methuselah what he had to do on his first date and what to do at a later stage, if he found the woman had an interest in him.

"Thank you so much, Leslie. At least now I can go for my date with confidence. What would I have done if I haven't met you?"

"What are friends for?" Leslie said. "Anytime you are not sure of anything, come and ask. I am not an expert, but I will do my best to help you."

"God bless you for being there for me when I needed you," Methuselah reiterated.

On that note they parted because it was getting late. Methuselah was quite satisfied with the information he got from Leslie, and he felt relieved that he hadn't become too apprehensive about what to say or do on his first date.

CHAPTER 14

The First Date

On Saturday, Methuselah got himself ready for the date. He looked smart in his best clothes. He walked to the river near the Apes as arranged. The day was bright, and as he stood looking down the river, the water was crystal clear. Methuselah enjoyed the beauty of nature, and the air he breathed was as fresh as a daisy. All around him was lovely and green, and some trees were very colourful because it was time for most flowers to bloom.

Kim arrived about thirty minutes late. By then, Methuselah was beginning to panic, wondering what could have gone wrong. Just as that went through his mind, he turned to his left and saw her approach. With excitement he walked towards her direction.

"Hey, baby! It's great to see you!"

"Hi, Methuselah. I do apologise for being late. Something cropped up just before I sat off, and I had to try to resolve it," Kim said.

"No need to apologise, darling. It's great that you could make it. Are you well?" he asked, putting his hand over Kim's shoulder.

"I am good. What about you, Methuselah?"

"I feel good now that you are here. To be honest, I am over the moon. I feel honoured to be with you today on such a beautiful day. You know what? This past week I have spent quite a few sleepless nights thinking about you, and I have been looking forward to meeting you today."

"It's grand to learn that you have been thinking about me," Kim said with a smile.

"Oh, Kim, you have such a beautiful smile. In fact, you are a stunning lady, and no man could resist you. I hope you don't mind me complimenting you."

"Not at all. Thanks for the compliments."

"Do you want to sit down by the Apes? Then we can relax, have a drink, talk, and get to know each other better."

"That sounds good, Methuselah. You know, with these high-heeled shoes, standing for too long one can be uncomfortable."

As they sat down, they discussed their interests and backgrounds. They both liked fishing, dogs, and going for walks. Methuselah and Kim were looking for a steady relationship, and neither wanted to mess around. After a lengthy discussion, he felt he had found the woman he was looking for, and he went on to make some proposals. By that time, they had had a few drinks because the Apes sold some beers and soft drinks. She was drinking Coke and Methuselah was into beer, but he made sure everything was still under control. Kim seemed to be the right woman for him.

"Kim, I am looking for true love, I was brought up as an orphan, and I feel it's time I found a woman who genuinely loves me."

"Oh! I am sorry, Methuselah. May I ask what exactly happened?"

"No, darling. This is not the right venue to discuss that. But I will tell you in the near future. Thanks all the same for showing concern; I do appreciate it."

On that note, Kim let herself fall into his loving arms. They cuddled each other and began kissing. For a few minutes, they did not say a word but continued enjoying this. Afterwards, Kim nestled her head into his neck whilst Methuselah whispered words of love into her ear. They enjoyed each other's company, and before they knew it, was 5 p.m. Kim's parents were very strict about arriving home late, and so she had to get home by 5.30.

"Methuselah, I have to go. Otherwise I will be in trouble with my parents," she said. "I don't want to go yet, but I have to be careful or else they won't allow me to go out again."

"Well, darling, I have enjoyed every minute with you, and I look forward to seeing you again. I hope it will be soon."

"Don't worry, it will be soon."

"Can I suggest a tentative date for us to meet again?"

"Oh! Yes, that's fine with me."

"What about next Saturday?"

"OK, we can meet next Saturday. But where?"

"Shall we meet at the Botswana border? Then we can catch a bus to Gaberone."

"That will be great fun, but it has to be quite early so we can be back on time," Kim suggested.

"Tell you what, darling. We will go for a nice meal, so don't eat anything before you come!"

"I am looking forward to that."

They agreed to meet at 9 a.m. at the Botswana border, and then they would take a bus to Gaberone. They hugged each other and kissed before they parted. It was a successful date for both of them because they were attracted to each other. Kim could not wait to tell her family she was very happy about her first date.

When Methuselah got home, he had tears of joy. He could not believe someone could fall for him.

The following morning, when he saw Leslie at work, he couldn't thank him enough for his support. "I thought I was completely useless when it comes to meeting a woman for the first time, but everything went well."

"You see? I told you that you would be fine," Leslie said.

"I suppose we'd better get on with work. We will talk a bit later," Methuselah said.

They went to their respective departments and continued to work hard as usual. Most people at work noticed that Methuselah was exceptionally happier, and the questions began.

"You seem jollier that usual today. Did anything good happen to you this weekend?" one of his workmates asked.

"Well, what do you expect me to say? Life can change overnight," Methuselah informed them.

"Whatever it is, it seems to have boosted your morale," another colleague commented.

"I am glad good things seem to be starting in my life. That's why you noticed. I will tell you more about it soon. For now, that's enough of my private life."

Everyone carried on with work and stopped discussing Methuselah's private life. During lunchtime, Methuselah sent some lunch for Kim because she was working at the other side, the Zimbabwean border. Kim was quite grateful when she got the lunch. She could see that she had met someone who was caring and considerate. In the evenings after work, Methuselah would walk Kim home but would leave her near the gate of their house.

It appeared everything had started going well for him at work and socially. While sitting in his home, he felt content about how life had taken such a good turn for him. At work he had been promoted, he had managed to build a nice small home for himself, and a beautiful woman had just come into his life. One night as he thought to himself, he knelt down to pray and thank God for what life had unexpectedly turned into. With everything going in his favour, he was a happy man.

Before his second date, he made an effort to relay the news to his grandparents on his mother's side; they were not very far from the Botswana border. When he arrived, they were quite surprised to see him during the middle of the week. They welcomed him as usual but were a bit worried about why he had decided to visit just like that.

"Is everything OK with you, Methuselah?" Grandma asked.

"Yes, Grandma, don't panic! I am only coming to tell you some good news."

"Great! What's the good news about?"

"I have met a woman I love, and it seems from the way things are going that she is attracted to me too."

"Thank God for that. At least that will put your mind at rest! I am happy for you, my grandson. Where does she live, and what's her name?"

"Her name is Kim. She lives with her parents near the Botswana border, but she is originally from Zimbabwe. She works for the Zimbabwe border."

"That's wonderful, son. We are thrilled to hear such news. At least if you have someone in your life. We don't have to worry about you so much. Well, what more would you want in life? You seem to be moving in the right direction," Granddad said.

Following the news, they had their evening meal, and it was a good meal to celebrate their grandson's success. Grandma fried some chicken served with some rice, and they bought some beer to make a toast. Methuselah and Granddad got drunk, but it was a special evening for them, and so no one was worried. They retired to bed quite early because Methuselah had to go to work the following morning.

In the morning, he woke up early to catch the first bus, which would get him to work on time. He returned back to work much happier because he had shared the good news with his grandparents. His grandparents also could not wait to see the other members of their family and tell them the exciting news about Methuselah.

CHAPTER 15

Trip to Gaberone

Methuselah and Kim met again as agreed. Kim arrived on time, and that meant a lot to Methuselah because it saved him from worrying about whether she was going to turn up. When one is in love everything has to happen on time, or else one is so quick to panic. As always, Methuselah was very excited to see Kim.

"Oh! Welcome, my angel!" he said, hugging Kim tightly. "I have missed you a lot."

"I have missed you too."

"As usual you are looking as glamorous as roses."

"Oh, thank you! You do know how to make a woman feel good, don't you?"

"But I mean what I say, darling. You are a beautiful lady. I am blessed to have you as my woman, and I thank God for meeting you."

"Thanks for your kind words. It's great when your man makes such comments about you."

They boarded a bus to Gaberone and sat at the back. Everyone in the bus could tell they were in love because they were cuddling and kissing all the way to Gaberone. Methuselah could not take his eyes off Kim; he looked at her in admiration all the way to Gaborone. He told her it felt like a dream that he had managed to get her.

"You know what, Kim? I am the happiest man since you came into my life."

"It's funny you should say that, because I feel the same."

"My life is now complete and I would not wish for anything else."

She said, "Well I consider myself lucky for finding a man who has so much passion and love for me."

"I love you very much, Kim, and I always will."

After spending time talking, kissing, and cuddling, they reached their destination. They let everyone get off first whilst they were still seated. As they got off the bus, they strolled hand in hand along the high street in Gaberone, trying to find a suitable place to have a meal. Finally they got to a Holiday Inn, which was one of the best hotels in the area, a five-star place. As they entered the hotel, they found that everything about it was beautiful, and it was perfect for a romantic outing. There was a restaurant as well as a bar.

First they decided to have a meal. Before the meal, they were served drinks. Methuselah had a pint of beer whilst Kim had a bottle of Coke. After that, they were given the menu, which provided a variety of meals including foreign dishes.

"Darling, the choice is yours. Price is not an issue."

"Thanks, love. I will have sirloin steak and chips, if that's okay with you," Kim said.

"Of course. Have whatever you want. I think I will have the same."

As soon as they were ready, the waiter came to take their orders. Methuselah ordered another beer whilst Kim opted for a glass of water.

"Make the steak well done please," Methuselah requested.

"OK, sir. It will come as per your request," the waiter answered.

The meal came as requested. Both of them were shy to eat because it was their first time to have a meal together. Eventually they got over that and enjoyed their meal. The steak was very nice and mouth-watering.

"Are you enjoying the meal? Do you need anything else?" the waiter asked.

"The meal is fantastic, and we are both enjoying it," Methuselah informed the waiter.

He paid for the meal, and they moved on to the bar for a chat and some more drinks. Kim continued to drink Coke whilst Methuselah drank beer. Both were relaxed and enjoyed caressing each other. It was a day to remember because it was their first proper outing since they'd first met.

Kim looked at the time and reminded Methuselah she had to head back home. "Thanks for a lovely meal. I thoroughly enjoyed it."

"Don't mention it, darling. It has been a great day, and I enjoyed every minute of it. You mean so much to me, and I am so happy in your company."

"Methuselah you are everything to me and I feel more like a woman since I met you."

Life couldn't get any better for Methuselah and Kim, who seemed to get on well as a couple. They walked to the bus station, moving slowly and speaking words of love. It was a day filled with great memories and a sense of belonging to each other. When they got to the bus station, they entered the bus and continued whispering words of love to each other.

"You know what, darling? Life is full of surprises. One minute I thought I had nobody, but it seems you are a godsend. You came at the right time."

"So did you, Methuselah. My life was incomplete without you."

"Kim, I love you now and always will."

When they reached their destination, Methuselah walked Kim home, up to the gate as he usually did. When they got to the gate, Kim insisted that he come inside to meet her family. Methuselah was a bit nervous about taking that step, but he knew it was for the best. He pulled himself together and went in to meet Kim's family.

"Mum and Dad, meet Methuselah, my boyfriend. Methuselah, meet my mum and dad, as well as my brother, Oliver, and my sister, Jennifer."

Methuselah said, "Pleased to meet you, Mum, Dad, Oliver, and Jennifer. It's my pleasure to meet you all."

"Please feel at home. We have heard a lot about you, Methuselah." Kim's mum said.

Kim's parents informed Methuselah that they were more than happy to meet him. He felt very welcome, stayed for a while, and then said he had to go because it was getting late. He refused anything to eat because they had already had something at the hotel. "I have to go now because I will be going to church in the morning."

"Okay, Methuselah. Thanks for coming. Take care of yourself, and see you soon," Kim's mum said.

"Don't forget to bring me some sweets next time you come," Jennifer said.

"Certainly, Jennifer. I will remember. You are such a sweet girl, aren't you?"

Kim, followed by Jennifer, went to see Methuselah at the gate. As they patted, Kim and Methuselah kissed and said goodbye. When they were kissing, Jennifer made a comment.

"I am going to tell Mum and Dad that you were kissing, and both of you will get a good hiding!"

Kim and Methuselah looked at each other and started laughing. After that, Methuselah proceeded home.

"It's not funny, Kim. I am going to tell Mum and Dad!"

"Jennifer, stop being silly, and don't talk rubbish."

"If I tell Mum and Dad, you will get into trouble."

"Oh, shush! Jennifer, you and your big mouth."

When they went inside the house, the first thing Jennifer did was report about Kim and Methuselah kissing. When Oliver heard, he advised Kim not to take Jennifer with her anymore. Mum and Dad told Jennifer to mind her own business and to be quiet. Jennifer was not very happy about those comments and sulked for the evening.

"Don't ask me to do anything for you again," Jennifer said to her mum.

"Oh, get lost Jennifer. We have had enough of you tonight. Go to bed now," Mum said with a raised tone.

Methuselah could not get over what had transpired. He was happy that the relationship was going better than he'd ever hoped. He thought that Kim's family were nice, and he was fortunate to meet such good people. The following morning, he went to church as per usual. When church finished, on his way home he saw Leslie, his best friend. He was so happy to see him and couldn't wait to break the news of his outing.

"You know what, Leslie? I am going through a phase in life where everything is going in my favour."

"I am happy for you, my friend. I am sure you deserve the best in life."

"Meeting Kim was the best thing that has ever happened to me. She is such a beautiful woman, full of love and commitment. I am very lucky to get someone like her."

"Methuselah, after what you have gone through, you deserve the best."

"Leslie, I appreciate your support. You will always be a great friend."

As they had talked, they decided to go Methuselah's place for something to eat and drink. Leslie felt good that he had been there for his friend at the time he'd needed him most. Once they finished eating, his friend decided to leave because he had to go to work the following morning. When Leslie left, Methuselah got his clothes ready for work in the morning. He went to sleep quite content with his progress.

CHAPTER 16

Meeting the Family

Methuselah took his girlfriend to meet his grandparents at Biet Bridge. His girlfriend was dressed to kill for the occasion. She wore a lovely, colourful dress with a low neckline, and it had a slit at the back. She also wore some beads and earrings to match the dress. On arrival, all members of the family were there, including his aunt, his uncle, and their families. Kim could not believe her eyes when she saw the number of family members waiting to meet her. At first she was a bit shy, but soon she pulled herself together.

Methuselah introduced Kim to his family, and they gave her a warm welcome. It appeared they were quite stunned about her beauty, and Granddad commented upon this.

"Well, son, you have certainly found yourself a beautiful woman."

"Thanks, Granddad. I am a lucky man indeed."

Grandma was filled with joy and started dancing and singing traditional songs. She appeared drunk, but it was just joy that she was expressing. Aunt Violet and Uncle Denise were over the moon about their nephew having found someone with whom he could share his future.

The family prepared some nice food to celebrate with Methuselah and his girlfriend. Granddad sent Denise to buy some beer for a toast, and they happily celebrated the occasion. Kim was quite impressed by what was happening, and she felt that it was genuine love.

Her boyfriend stood up after they had finished eating and made a short speech. "Kim, as I told you before, I became an orphan at twelve years, Grandma and Granddad brought me up. Always bear in mind that these are what I call my parents. I hope you will always give them the respect they deserve. I am what I am because of their love and commitment."

Everyone listened to his speech and was touched by his words. When he finished, he decided it was time for him and his girlfriend to catch the bus. Kim also expressed her appreciation for such a warm welcome and for the meal. Before Kim left, she told them that she would always remember the day.

The rest of the family saw them off at the bus stop. As they bade them farewell, the bus came, and Methuselah and his girlfriend got on. On the way, they discussed the day's events and were content with everything. Kim cuddled Methuselah, kissed him, and thanked him for a lovely day.

"You know what, darling? You have a wonderful family full of love and care."

"Thanks, Kim. They have always loved and cared for me so much since I lost my parents. I could not have wished for anything better. I still wish my parents were here, but my grandparents have done their best to give me love and care to keep me going. Further, I feel I owe them a lot. Time will tell how I will compensate for all they have done for me."

"But, darling, what they have done is all out of love and in good faith. They might not expect anything back. All they want is for you to be happy."

"Thanks, Kim. You are right. I am grateful for your kind words."

After the conversation, they got off the bus. Methuselah walked his girlfriend to the gate and then headed to his place. When she got home, Kim was full of praise for the good welcome she'd received from her boyfriend's family. In particular, she could not get over Grandma singing and dancing.

Later, Kim's parents went to their bedroom and discussed how they felt about their future son-in-law. They felt he was a steady, good-looking person who seemed to be committed to their daughter. They were sympathetic to him being an orphan, but they were aware that their daughter was a kind and caring person who would look after him well. What they were mostly concerned about was doing the best by their lovely daughter, and they did not want anything to go wrong in her life. After a lengthy talk about their daughter's affairs, they went to sleep.

In her bedroom, Kim was still awake and unable to stop thinking about her boyfriend. She thought he was a godsend and could not wait for Monday, when she could see him again. Finally she fell asleep, but it was quite late.

Kim woke up very late the following day, and her parents were getting concerned because she was usually an early bird. Jennifer tried to wake her up twice, but Kim still went back to sleep again. Later, she woke up just in time for lunch.

"What time do you call this you, lazy bugger?" Jennifer said.

"Eh, mind your language. You don't speak to Kim like that," Mum told Jennifer.

"Mum, you always tell me off for waking up late. What about Kim?"

"For you it's an everyday problem, whereas for Kim it's only today."

"Oh! I give up on you, Mum. You always blame me for everything!"

"That's enough from you, Jennifer. It's time you realise you don't speak to your elders in that tone."

When Mum finished talking, Jennifer went quiet and realised that Mum was no longer going to take any of her nonsense. After that, Mum served lunch for all members of the family, which they thoroughly enjoyed. That day she had cooked some lamb stew served with rice and cabbage. There was division of labour, and so Dad went to do some gardening after lunch. Mum and the girls continued with the housework and then started preparing for the evening meal. Jennifer and her brother did their homework in preparation for school the following morning.

Kim's family lived in town, and it appeared their lifestyle was more modern than Methuselah's family's, who were of a rural background. Nevertheless, when Kim visited her boyfriend's family, she quite enjoyed the way everything was done and did not find any problems with their lifestyle. She saw it as a learning process for her.

CHAPTER 17

Back at Sarowe Village, Ramie's Wife Was Taken by Force

Ten years after Sithu's and Bayeme's deaths, the chief continued treating villagers unkindly. This time there was a different issue. A long time ago, he had fallen for Ramie's wife and had to find some way to make her his own. As usual he would go around the village to make sure everything was OK. In a way, his rounds were not genuine because he was monitoring the woman he fancied and talking to her more often to suit his sexual desires. He continued bumping into Liana, the woman he liked very much.

Liana was the wife of Ramie, one of the villagers. She was in her mid-twenties and was admired by most men in the village because she was an attractive woman. Her husband thought the world of her and felt a bit insecure at times. Chief Muyabwo met her a few times and would stop and talk to her. One day the chief sent his men, Barry and Togo, to bring Liana to his place because he wanted to have a word with her. His men got to the woman's house, and her husband was there. They asked if they could have a word with them both inside the house because what they were going to say was private and confidential. After a few minutes, they said why they had been sent.

"We have been sent by the chief to bring your wife, Liana, to his place," one of the men said.

"For what reason would he want to see my wife?" Ramie asked.

"She will let you know as soon as she gets back."

"Please don't let the chief take my wife. I love her very much, and I would not want anyone to take her from me," Ramie cried. "If that's the case, I will have to come with you because I don't trust what you are going to do with my wife. If the chief has to kill me, then he will have to do it today."

"Ramie, please don't waste our time, as well as yours. You are aware that we are only messengers," the chief's men said.

"I know you are messengers, but that is my wife we are talking about, and I have a right to protect her!"

"Ramie, the chief only wants to see Liana. Please, we beg you to stay behind and wait for your wife to come and report whatever transpires."

"OK, I will stay. But it had better not be too long, or else I shall be at the chief's door."

"To hell with the chief. I am not leaving my husband," Liana reiterated. "I love my husband and will not let anything separate us."

"We'll see when we get there what he has to say," said the messengers.

The chief's men took Liana with them even though she protested. She had tears running down her cheeks all the way to the chief's place. She knew the chief had taken a shine to her because he had stopped a few times to talk to her whenever he was making his rounds. Deep down in her heart, she knew if that was the case, her husband would not stand a chance to prevent that from happening.

When they arrived at the chief's place, he was waiting. She was taken straight to the chief's private room, where he would not be disturbed.

"Liana, I have called you to let you know you are a beautiful woman, and I have been admiring you for some time."

"How could that be? I am already somebody's wife. I love my husband, and he loves me too. I don't have any feelings for you and would never dream of being in love with you."

"Well, I am in control of everybody, and no one can question what I do."

"Please don't do that to me. I want to go back and be with my husband," Liana insisted.

"I think you are wasting your time, as well as mine. I don't go back on my decisions."

"What's going to happen to my husband?"

"I will not have him killed, but I will ask him to move from this village."

"Oh, my Lord. We are a young couple recently married with the intentions of having children soon."

"From today onwards, you are my wife. I will send my men to collect your clothes and whatever is any value to you. As for your husband, I will summon him and tell him to leave this village with immediate effect."

"Where is he going to go? He has lived in this village all his life," she said.

"That's nothing to do with me. All I want is you, and I promise you will be very happy with me as your new husband."

"That's cruel! I do not think you should do this to people."

"Liana, that's enough. I won't continue tolerating any rubbish talk from you. I am going to send my men to bring your husband along so that I can let him know what my plan is for you."

She continued to cry, but that was not going to help the situation. The chief called one of his men to summon the husband. When they brought the husband, he was shaking with anger but knew very well he would not be able to prevent what the chief was going to do.

"Young man, I have summoned you because I want you to move from this village immediately."

"What about my wife? I love her very much. I don't want to go away without her," Ramie said.

"She is not yours anymore. She is mine, and she is going to be the happiest woman."

"I suppose life is unfair, and I have to take it that I am a loser," Ramie cried.

"You are lucky because I am asking you to move in one piece. Pack your stuff and vacate the village."

"Where am I going to go? You know I have always lived in this village."

"Go now and find somewhere to live—or else my men will show you where to go."

"Bye, Liana. As the chief says, I have to go, but only God knows where he will lead me."

Ramie left the chief's place sobbing, and his wife was also in tears. He went back home and packed all his clothes. He did not tell anyone about what had happened because he found it quite humiliating. Ramie was aware that there was nothing much that could be done about it, and he decided to leave the village peacefully even though he was very heartbroken. He went to live with his grandparents in a village about fifty miles from Sarowe.

Meanwhile, the chief's men went to collect Liana's belongings as per his instructions. She was allocated a house at the chief's place because he had a few empty houses. She struggled to live with what had happened to her and her husband, but she had to put up with it. She was in tears most of the time but eventually settled down. Liana knew if she attempted to run away, the chief would certainly find her, and she would probably lose her life.

The other villagers were not aware of what had taken place because they could only see Liana at the chief's place. The husband left in the night and did not tell any one of his predicaments because he felt disgraced. Liana was not allowed to talk about it, per the chief's instruction. The villagers were thus left guessing what had transpired. The day they'd seen the chief's men at Liana's house, they could tell something was not right.

With time, Liana got pregnant by the chief and had a baby boy named Theo. She became the chief's favourite wife. He had four wives, the most recent being Liana. She had maids working for her, and the chief would do anything to keep her happy because she was the youngest of the wives. Strangely enough, all the chief's wives got on very well because he would not allow any animosity amongst them.

As for Ramie, no one knew what happened to him. He was so hurt and did not want anything to do with anyone at Sarowe. He had nobody to visit in the village because his parents had moved from there a few years back. From the night he'd been told to move away, he kept a distance.

CHAPTER 18

Methuselah and Kim Spend the Night Together

Two years later, Methuselah and Kim were lovers, and the relationship was going smoothly. He decided to invite his girlfriend to spend a night with him, and on that night he was going to make his proposal for marriage. On the Friday two weeks before the day, as they were having their lunch at work, he asked Kim to stay over. He knew it was not normally allowed but thought it was time they do so.

"Darling, I have been thinking about this for a while. I want us to spend a night together at my place, if that's okay with you."

"How are we going to tell my parents?"

"That's why it took me time to ask you about this. It's not going to be easy, but there is always a way to go around it."

"Yes, I would love to spend a night with you—if you can come up with how we are going to make it happen."

"What about if we tell a bit of porky pies? Pretend you are going to spend the night with your aunt, and then we talk to your aunt. That's what we are going to do."

"That might be a way forward. My aunt trusts you, and I am sure she will do anything for you."

"Great! Shall we go and see your aunt after work?"

"Okay, we'll do that and hope for the best."

After lunch, they went back to their departments. Methuselah could not stop thinking about it and could only hope the plan would work. At the same time, Kim had not done this before and was quite anxious to make that move. But on the other hand, she loved Methuselah so much and was prepared to do anything to make this work.

After work, they met as arranged and took a walk to see Kim's aunt. Kim's aunt was surprised to see them arriving at that time, around 6 p.m.

"Is everything okay? What has brought this visit at this time of the evening?"

"Aunt, don't worry. We have something we want to discuss with you in confidence," Methuselah said.

She welcomed them and made them something to eat whilst they discussed the issue of their visit. She agreed that she would do them a favour, hoping that Kim's parents would not find out. Methuselah and Kim were quite happy that their plans were going to work out. Later, they headed home, and as usual Methuselah took Kim home first.

As the sleepover weekend approached, Methuselah prepared for the occasion by buying groceries and drinks and also making sure the house was nice and clean. It was as if he was preparing for the coming of the queen. The house was spotless, and he looked his best. He was so excited and could not wait for her arrival. At about 4 p.m., he looked through the window and saw Kim approaching. With excitement he opened the door and gave her a warm welcome.

"Welcome, darling. Come in and make yourself at home. I have been longing for this day, Kim."

"Me too, Methuselah. I am glad it all worked out for us to spend the night together."

After a little while, Methuselah started cooking whilst Kim sipped a drink he had given her. He was a good cook, and that night he made fried steak, rice, and spring cabbage. When they finished eating, they sat in the lounge and relaxed over a glass of white wine. Kim complimented Methuselah's cooking, saying the food was lovely and she enjoyed it very much. Strangely enough, Kim had some wine that night, but only a small glass. She was not used to drinking, and that small glass made her tipsy.

Before they went to sleep, Methuselah made a proposal to Kim. "Kim, I have something important to say to you, which is why I wanted to spend more time with you."

"What is it, darling?" Kim asked with a lot of excitement.

"I have known you long enough, and I feel it's time we should settle down. In short, I want to marry you. Will you marry me?"

She went tongue tied and didn't know what to say. Then she blurted, "Yes, I will! I will marry you, Methuselah! You know I love you very much, and my love for you will never change." Tears of joy ran down her cheeks because she was overwhelmed by the great news.

"Thanks, Kim. I consider myself a very lucky man indeed to find a beautiful woman like you. I promise I will always be loyal to you and give you all the happiness you can find in a man."

Following acceptance of his proposal, Methuselah gave Kim a big cuddle and kissed her. He said he was the happiest man in the world and continued to say he had found a wife as well as a mother. They agreed for the big occasion to take place in four weeks' time. Because it was an African marriage, Methuselah had to pay lobola to Kim's parents. Lobola was some form of money paid to the woman's parents to thank them for raising their daughter. After their lengthy discussion, they went to sleep. They enjoyed each other in bed, and certainly that was the night they both lost their virginity.

The following day, they prepared to go to Kim's aunt to inform her of their intention to get married. When she heard the news, she was very happy for them and could not wait to tell Kim's parents. Kim and Methuselah spent most of the day with Kim's aunt as she prepared a nice meal to celebrate their good news. Later, they thanked her for letting them spend the night together and for all the support she gave them.

When they had gone, Kim's aunt started making plans to let Kim's parents know about the big event. She decided she was going to visit them the following day. She broke the news to them because they needed time to let their close relatives know, and they also needed as much time as possible to prepare for the event.

CHAPTER 19

The Family Discovers the Good News

Methuselah visited both sets of grandparents on two successive days after work. They lived in areas quite distant from each other. On a Monday after work, he saw his grandparents on his mother's side, who were surprised to see him arrive because he had not seen them for a while.

"Is there a problem with you, my son? We haven't seen you for a while," Grandma said.

"No, Grandma. I am coming to tell you of the good news."

"Oh? What is it, my son? Are you getting married to that angel?"

"Yes, Grandma. How did you know?"

"That is the only great news I can think about presently. Congratulations, my son! We are all happy for you because you deserve some happiness. When is the big day? Granddad will have to be involved in the discussions of lobola."

"It will be four weeks from now. That will be on Saturday, 30 September."

"Please make sure you come on the Friday before the day so you can discuss with Granddad what's expected of you on that day."

"I will do so, Grandma. You know I need every piece of advice I can get from you. Once again, thanks for everything, you two. I will always cherish your love and care."

Granddad gave him a hug, and Grandma gave him kiss and a hug. Then she started singing for joy. As usual, she appeared to be drunk whenever she was happy. This was an event where it was time to sing the traditional songs and dance to celebrate. Later, she settled and then requested everyone be present to join her in prayer. It appeared she was quite a character, but she certainly knew how to express herself when she was happy. Most people who knew her were always fascinated at the way she expressed her happiness whenever she got a piece of good news.

When they had eaten their supper, they retired early because their grandson had to go to work in the morning. Before Methuselah went to sleep, he bade farewell to his grandparents because he was not going to see them in the morning.

He woke up very early in the morning, around 5 a.m., to catch a bus. It was a lovely morning: birds sang, and the sun was just rising. The breeze was as cool as a cucumber. Methuselah walked to the bus stop, enjoying the gift of nature and appreciating its beauty. Deep down he was so excited and looking forward to his big day. As far as he was concerned, it was the best time in his life. He felt he had found true love.

At work, he told all his workmates and his bosses, who were all happy for him. His workmates and his friends made some plans to take him out for a drink the weekend before the event. Meanwhile, Kim's workmates were all happy for her and planned to take her out before the day. Kim's family was thrilled about the news, and all arrangements required for the event were put in place well in time. African beer was brewed a few days before the event, and some traditional dancers were invited to celebrate the day.

After work, Methuselah rushed to board a bus to go to his other grandparents on his father's side. He respected both sets of his grandparents and treated them equally. As soon as he got there, they were astonished to see him arriving at the beginning of the week.

"Is everything okay, son? What brings you at this time of the evening?"

"Everything is fine, Ma. I am coming to let you know I will soon be a grown man. I am getting married on 30 September."

"Oh! Congratulations, Grandson. We are all pleased for you and are delighted to know you now have a best friend in life. We are looking forward to the big day."

They had their evening meal and discussed what Methuselah needed to prepare for the day. He was only too happy to take all the guidance he could get from his grandparents. Following their discussion, they retired early because Methuselah had to catch the earliest bus again.

CHAPTER 20

Getting Married the Traditional Way

On 30 September, both families gathered for the big occasion. Any gatherings required before the day were carried out, and every member was set for the day. It was a beautiful day: the sky was blue, and the weather was as fresh as a daisy. It appeared that most members of Kim's family were as busy as bees, trying to make sure that everything went according to plan and that all the guests were well received and well fed.

Kim looked more angelic than ever, and any time she glanced at anyone, they could not help but notice that she was a beautiful woman and that Methuselah was a lucky guy. Furthermore, Methuselah felt on top of the moon to know that everyone was gathered together to celebrate his and Kim's day. Whenever he looked at Kim, he could not believe that it was real. Around ten in the morning, it was time for the function to start, and everyone who was present had had some breakfast and was set for the occasion.

The traditional singers and dancers started the ball rolling by singing and dancing, and those who were present enjoyed watching them dance and sing. The female traditional dancers wore very low-cut tops, showing their boobs, and they had some heavy beads around their necks and ankles. Further, they wore short flared skirts with very colourful beads at the bottom. The male dancers were topless and wore similar skirts to the ladies. Like the ladies, their skirts were flared and short, and as they danced, their pants and knickers showed. Nobody was bothered because the whole idea was to entertain those who had gathered for the occasion.

At 10.15, both families gathered together under a tree, and there were chairs and tables available for all members. Kim's father and his brothers sat at the front. Kim, her mother, and her mother's sisters and her father's sisters sat behind them. On the other side were Methuselah and his grandparents, his aunt, and his uncle. Kim's uncle spoke first.

"Welcome to the occasion we all been waiting for. Are you all happy that Kim and Methuselah are marrying today? It is indeed a wonderful feeling that we are gathered to celebrate their wonderful day."

As he finished his opening remarks, everyone present started clapping, and those who could whistle did so as a sign of cheer. After the opening remarks, it was time to start making the charges, as per the African culture. Methuselah had saved reasonable money to meet all that was culturally required. There were several charges, including clothing for both Kim's parents, some monies that would be used to buy a herd of cattle, and more. When that was all over and money from Methuselah had been laid on the table, it was time for everyone to start dancing and celebrating. As far as African culture was concerned, Methuselah and Kim were now husband and wife. That also meant that Methuselah could take his wife with immediate effect, if he wanted to.

But both Kim and Methuselah were both Christians, and had invited the priest to bless them once the traditional requirements were met. The priest blessed their marriage, and it was time for the bride to kiss the bridegroom, which was the moment Methuselah and Kim had been waiting for. After that, everybody continued to celebrate and make big cheers of joy.

People ate, drank, and were merry. For Methuselah's grandparents, it was a special day mixed with happiness and sadness. They felt sadness because they missed Methuselah's parents on that special occasion. But on that particular day, they tried to put on brave faces so that no one could realise what they were going through. His grandmother on his mother's side went on to perform her special dance, and she requested to sing her special song to celebrate for her grandson. Everybody cheered for her when she finished her performance. She asked to give a short speech and was given the go-ahead.

"Please allow me to express my gratitude to Kim and Methuselah, and to thank them for what they have done today. Today, Methuselah, you have found yourself a best friend as well as mother. Kim, we take you as our daughter, and we will always have a lot of respect for you as long as we live. This is a great day for all of us, and we feel our prayers have been answered."

When she finished, there was much cheering from Kim's family because they believed that their daughter was highly valued. Kim gave her a hug and a big kiss, and Methuselah did the same. The day continued with lots to eat and drink, as well dancing. Methuselah and Kim started dancing together to celebrate their day. Everybody admired them because they suited each other so well.

Once the ceremony was over, all who had gathered dispersed except the bride and the bridegroom, who were still celebrating in style. They left for their honeymoon immediately after the ceremony.

CHAPTER 21

Honeymoon at the Victoria Falls

After the ceremony, Kim and Methuselah had their clothes packed to go to the Victoria Falls. They took their entire luggage and went to board the bus to Bulawayo. They'd take a connecting bus to the Victoria Falls. Bulawayo was the second biggest city in Zimbabwe, and Victoria Falls was one of the beautiful tourist places. It was situated at the border of Zimbabwe and Zambia. Kim was a Zimbabwean and had always wanted to visit the Victoria Falls. While they were on the bus to Bulawayo, they were full of excitement, and the feeling of belonging to each other for life was enough to make their life complete. They were kissing and cuddling and appeared to be in their own world, forgetting about other passengers who were looked at them as if they were watching a love film.

"Kim, I feel like I am in a dream, having you as my wife."

"Darling, this is a dream come true for both of us."

"Life is now more meaningful. Thanks to God for blessing me with a beautiful wife."

As they talked, they felt closer to each other than they had ever felt before. Before they knew it, they arrived in Bulawayo, and it was time to change for the bus to take them to the Victoria Falls. When they got off, some people made comments about them being in love, but they ignored them and went to the next bus. By this time, it was near 8.30 p.m., and Kim was getting tired because it had been such a long day for her. Her husband saw this and offered to carry her on his back, but she refused and smiled at him. Once she realised that the offer was genuine, she tried to pull herself together and pretended that she was OK.

They arrived at the next bus station to board a bus to Victoria Falls. The place seemed deserted because there were no people travelling around that time of the night. Kim and Methuselah got on the bus and looked for a comfortable seat where they could sleep. The seats were adjustable because these buses were for travelling long distances. Once they sat down, Methuselah couldn't wait to take Kim into his hands and lay her head on his shoulder.

"I know you are tired, my darling. Try to relax and have some rest."

"But it has been a long day for you too. You must feel as tired as I do."

"Don't worry about me, darling, I am concerned about you being comfortable, my angel."

"Thanks, Methuselah. You are a very caring husband."

The bus drove fast, and it took them about five hours to get to the Victoria Falls. When they arrived at the hotel, the porters took their luggage into their room whilst they checked in. They were glad to arrive because it was now the early hours of the morning. The first thing they did when they got into their room was have a shower to freshen themselves before seducing each other into lovemaking. They both looked forward to lovemaking without worrying about anybody else.

"Kim, I will do the honours of washing your back, I have been dying to wash your back. Oh! You have very smooth skin, and you have a fantastic body."

As he continued to explore his wife's body, he couldn't wait to get into bed with her. Finally they got into bed and enjoyed lovemaking and being able to spend a night together freely. It was a night to remember as they enjoyed each other often. After a while, they both went to sleep and did not get up till eight in the morning, when some tea was brought to their room.

"What a wonderful night, darling. I really enjoyed you."

"Me too, Methuselah. You are such a good lover, enough to drive anyone crazy."

"I am glad we both enjoyed each other because that is very important to any marriage. Kim, I love you very much and want you to be happy with everything I do to you."

They had their cup of tea and decided to rest in bed, caressing each other. They could not stop whispering words of love to each other, and they had on some lovely music in the background. It was the best time in their lives, and love was the food of life. Later, they woke up, had a bath, and then went to the restaurant to eat some breakfast.

Soon after breakfast, they decided to go for a walk. Victoria Falls was full of beauty. The forests were green and colourful, and the falls were the best for any human eye to see. Kim and Methuselah could not get over the beauty of nature at the falls.

"Oh, Methuselah. Look at the lovely rainbow. Isn't that fabulous?"

"Darling, I am glad we decided to come here for our honeymoon because it is a great place full of nature's beauty."

"My word! Have you seen those lovely animals drinking water just behind the hotel? What an amusing place to visit. This is a nice place for lovers. There is so much to see and enjoy together."

"Yes, you are right, Kim. We are having the greatest time of our lives."

Everything about Victoria Falls was a great experience for both of them. Neither of them had been exposed to such beauty in their past. Methuselah kept thanking Kim for choosing the falls for their honeymoon.

On their second day at the falls, they decided to go boating, which was another experience they found quite fascinating. The waters were crystal clear and very deep.

"Darling, we will have a lot to tell people, and I am sure it is an experience we will never forget as long as we live," Kim said.

"A honeymoon is an experience which should never be forgotten."

Time went quickly while they had fun. They were booked for one week, and before they knew it, the week was gone. They had to start packing to go back home. However, they were happy that everything about their visit to Victoria Falls was great. Though they were going back to the Botswana border, this time they would be living together as husband and wife. A day before going back, they went out shopping to get a few souvenirs and some presents for their close family members.

On Sunday morning, they checked out and got a bus to Bulawayo, which arrived at 1.30 p.m. Then they proceeded to the next bus for the Botswana border. They had to wait at least an hour before getting the next bus, but everything was okay as long as they had each other.

"Kim, it feels good to be married. Now we have each other for life."

"My darling, I hope we stay as close as we are now, because life couldn't be any better than this."

"Kim, don't forget that life is a journey, and we will not expect everything to go smoothly all the time. Everything will depend on how we handle what goes wrong. Anyway, we need not think of anything going wrong. I am determined to make our marriage work."

As they talked their next bus arrived, and they boarded it. When they settled on the bus, Methuselah cuddled his wife and kissed her every now and again. Most passengers looked at them. Some looked with admiration, and others felt they were showing off. That did not bother Methuselah and his wife.

In less than two hours, they arrived at the Botswana border, and they walked home to Methuselah's place, which was now Kim's new home.

"Here we are, Kim. Welcome to our home. Make yourself at home. Feel free to make any changes as it suits you, darling, I am happy to go with whatever you feel is better for our home."

"Thanks, Methuselah. You are so sweet and thoughtful. To be honest, the place looks good as it is. But I will still make one or two changes so that my presence can be felt."

They started unpacking their luggage, and then they had to get ready for bed because they were so tired from the long journey. At least they still had another week off work; they preferred to be at home and rest before going back to work. Also, Kim wanted to settle in her new home. She enjoyed every moment with her husband, and they were very fond of each other.

They spent the rest of the week doing things at home and visiting a few friends, such as Leslie and Kim's aunt, to give presents they'd brought back from Victoria Falls. Kim's aunt was more than pleased to see them back and receive the present. As for Leslie, he was quite happy that his friend was now so happy.

After their holidays were finished, they went back to work and had so much to tell the people there. All their friends and colleagues at work warmly welcomed them back. Most people were congratulating them because they had not seen them since they'd married.

"Did everything go according to plan, Methuselah?" Methuselah's boss asked.

"Everything went well. It has been eye opening and a great experience, and it feels good to be married. We have treasured every moment, and

Victoria Falls is a very nice place to visit. I tell you, I have never seen such a beautiful place."

On that note, Methuselah carried on with his work whilst his boss moved on to other things.

Kim continued to say a lot of good things about their honeymoon and also about how lucky she was to have married to Methuselah. She said she couldn't have wished for a better husband than Methuselah.

CHAPTER 22

A Voice Came for the Second Time

It happened on a Friday, when Methuselah and Kim had finished eating and were resting after a long day's work. They got ready for bed as usual and went to sleep. That particular night, Methuselah felt extra tired. As he slept, he heard a voice speaking. He recognised the voice and woke up immediately.

"Oh! The voice sounds like you, Father. Is it you?"

"Yes, my son. Don't be afraid. It's me, your father."

"Oh, Father, where are you? I can hear your voice, but I can't see you."

"My son, as I said before, you can't see me physically, but you can hear my voice. Your mother and I are very happy about your progress in life. I am glad that from the day I spoke to you, you are now standing like a man. We are also happy that God has now blessed you with a wife."

"How come I never seem to hear Mum's voice since she has died?"

"She is always looking over you and always praying to the Almighty to guide you in everything you do."

"Thank you, Dad. It is great to realise that you are looking over me in everything I do."

"My son, we left you so suddenly, and you were too young to cope with life's struggles. We thank the Almighty for the prayers well answered. I have one important task that I want you to carry out. I know this is going to be difficult, but I will guide you when the time comes."

"Carry on, Father. I am listening."

"I want you to take revenge! Revenge, revenge! I will guide you at a later stage regarding how to carry out the task."

"Whatever you say, Dad. I will follow your instructions."

"I will have to go now."

The voice left. For a few minutes, Methuselah felt emotional. He wanted to talk to his father for much longer, but because he was more mature, he had learnt to accept life as it came in all situations.

As that happened, Kim was listening and wondering what was going on with her husband. It appeared when Methuselah heard his father's voice, he got very involved in the conversation. That particular night, with Kim present, he had to be prepared to explain what was going on, although he was not to go into depth.

"Methuselah, what is going on, darling? I couldn't make out to whom you were talking. Were you talking in your sleep, or is it something that I am not meant to know?"

"Darling, I tend to hear my father once in a while, and this is quite real. You only have to be in my shoes to understand what this is all about."

"I am sorry if I am asking for too much information."

"No need to apologize, Kim. You are my wife and you have the right to ask about anything that goes on in my life. You know what? Until I started hearing my father's voice, I did not know that one can talk to the dead. Darling, I am going to tell you something that I have not revealed to anyone before. I want you to keep it to yourself."

"I will," she said.

"One time I became suicidal because I missed my parents. As I was about to throw myself in the river, a voice came from my father telling me to not commit suicide. From that time, I learnt to stand like a man, and I can face any problem like a man. So believe it or not, darling, the dead can talk to you when you are in crisis. Now I appreciate my father's voice talking to me that time, because I have my wife, whom I love very much. I am glad to be alive because I have a lot to live for, sweetheart. You understand why I will not ignore my father's voice."

"Yes, I fully understand, Methuselah. I love you very much, and I also thank your father's voice for stopping you from committing suicide."

Methuselah and Kim stayed awake for a while discussing what had happened to Methuselah in the past, but still he would not talk about the revenge. He was going to organise it without his wife knowing. Eventually Kim fell asleep, but Methuselah was still awake and thinking about how he was going to seek revenge.

As Dad said, it is not going to be an easy task. But he is going to guide me, and so I will have to follow his instructions. Whatever I do, I have to play my cards right because I don't want to mess up my wife.

He finally went back to sleep, thanking God that the following day was a Saturday, and he did not have to wake up too early.

CHAPTER 23

The Voice Is Heard for the Third Time

It was six months after Methuselah had heard the voice at night. During this time, Kim was visiting her parents, and for some reason Methuselah had decided to stay behind on his own. At 1.30 a.m., he heard someone calling his name, and he woke up in a state but realised that it could be his father's voice.

"Methuselah! Methuselah, can hear me?"

"Yes, Father, I am listening."

"I thought since you are on your own, it might be the best time to talk. I come to give you the instructions about how you can go about the revenge. You have to listen to me carefully and do exactly as I tell you, because doing it on your own is not an easy task."

"Okay, Father. I am your vessel. Use me the way you want. I will follow your instructions."

"I want you to go to the Gaberone bus station the following Saturday morning, around ten. You will see two dreadlocked men wearing black attire. Those are the guys to talk to. When you get to them, I will bring strong winds within that area to show you that you are at the right spot. These guys have guns and can do anything for money, but do not worry because they will not harm you. My spirit will be with you. They operate as a gang with other guys. Once you approach them, start talking to the guys who can carry out the mission. They will not charge you too much money because I will make sure their hearts are not hardened. All you have to do is to talk to them about the charges and set the date to carry out the revenge. You do not have to do anything apart from showing them where Chief Muyabwo resides. Did you understand all I have said?"

"I understand every word you said, and I will do as you command."

"Remember, my son. Your mother and I died prematurely, and you struggled as an orphan, which you did not deserve."

"Yes, Father! I will not forget. Your death left a wound within me which will never heal." Then he burst into tears.

"No! No, Methuselah, I do not want you to cry. I want you to be as brave as a lion. Get revenge!"

All of a sudden, the voice disappeared, and he continued to digest all that had been said. He spent most of the weekend deliberating what he was going to do the following weekend. At the same time, he had to be secretive about the revenge. The last thing he wanted was for his wife to know about the plot to get revenge. At the same time, he felt guilty for not telling her because he had always been open with his wife regarding everything else since he'd first met her. But as far as he was concerned, this had to be done or else he would feel disloyal to his father.

Later that Sunday afternoon, Kim came back from her weekend leave. Methuselah was happy to see her back, but Kim could see that there was something bothering him. "Darling, you are not quite yourself. Is there something wrong?"

"No, Kim, I am fine. But sometimes I do tend to think of how my parents died. I don't want to deliberate on the past so much because it spoils our happiness as a couple."

"Never mind, darling. I will try my best to give you all the support that you need, so don't feel that you are on your own."

"Thanks, Kim. You are God given. That is why I love you so much. God has given me a wife as well as my best friend, as I have said before."

"Anyway, darling did you have a nice weekend?"

"It was great, but I missed you so much."

"Oh! Bless you. I also missed you terribly."

After the welcome, Kim went to the kitchen to start preparing the evening meal. When they finished eating, they retired to bed because Methuselah had to go to work in the morning. Methuselah tossed and turned but pretended to be sleeping; it appeared he was not going to have peace of mind until the mission was accomplished.

For the whole week before Methuselah met those guys who were going to carry out the mission, Kim could tell that her husband was not quite himself, and he just presented a picture of something not being right. She did not want to keep asking questions because she knew from past experience that her husband would not hide anything from her. But on this particular incident, it appeared he had to hide what he was going to do because he had also hidden this from his grandparents.

The following Saturday, Methuselah got a bus to the Gaberone bus stop, as per his father's instruction. He arrived there on time, and as he approached the two men, there came very strong winds. He was assured that his father was with him in spirit. At the same time, the two men were in black and had some dreads.

"Hi, guys. I am Methuselah."

"Hi. Can we help you with anything?"

"I need to talk to you something very confidential."

"Go on, then. We are listening."

"Can you do me a favour?"

"It depends what it is about, because whatever it is it depends on your pocket."

"Well, guys, this is all about what happened to me in the past. My parents were hanged in Sarowe village by Chief Muyabwo, and I want to take revenge. I need some help to carry out this revenge. Obviously he is a very strong man, and I cannot carry out this revenge without a gun."

"As we said, we can do anything—as long as you can pay us good money."

"How much will you charge for that?"

"About 1,200 pula. Can you afford that?"

"Could you make it any cheaper than that, please?"

"This is what we call danger money, and we expect it to be paid up front before we carry out the mission. Pay us 1,100 pula, and we can do this for you. When do you want this done, and when can you pay us?"

"Would you be able to do it next Saturday around 4 a.m.? I suspect the chief and his family will be at home."

"That is a deal. When can you pay us?"

"I will give you the money before we set off for Sarowe village. Where can we meet?"

"We can meet here. We will drive, and you will be responsible for putting fuel in the car. Is that okay?"

"Thanks, guys. I will see you next Saturday."

After talking to these men, Methuselah felt that it was a mission accomplished. However, he was worried about what explanation to give to his wife about where he had been. Also, he was concerned about what explanation to give for the following Saturday, when he had to be there very early. He felt the best way would be to tell his wife he was going to his grandparents on a Friday night and then take it from there.

As soon as he got home, he explained to his wife that he was required to sort out something at his grandparents' place in Beit Bridge, and he had to go on a Friday and spend the night with them. Kim could sense that something was going on, but she did not want her husband to feel uncomfortable, and so she refrained from asking too many questions.

CHAPTER 24

Bloodshed at Sarowe Village

On Saturday, in the early part of the morning, Methuselah met with the gangsters as arranged. They met at 3.30 and set off after he gave them the monies they had requested. It was a team of eight guys who were all dressed in black, wearing black sunglasses and black gloves. They drove a big black van with tinted windows. They drove quite fast, and in about thirty minutes they arrived. Action began as one knocked on the door, and the rest were still hiding in the black van.

"What are you doing, knocking on my door at this time of the morning?"

"Well, this is just the time we thought we would find you," one of the gangster answered.

"What is this, then Is it a plot to kill me?"

"You said it," the gangster answered.

"What have I done wrong?"

"Do you remember Sithu and Bayeme?"

"What has that to do with you?" the chief asked.

"We have their son, Methuselah, who has come to seek revenge."

Methuselah shouted with anger, "Yes! Yes, Chief Muyabwo. You killed my parents years back. Today, it's your turn!"

"Please, Methuselah, don't kill me. I will give you anything."

"That was the plea I said that day when you hung my parents, and you were not prepared to listen. My parents died prematurely because of your cruelty. Today, Chief Muyabwo, you are finished. What goes around comes around!"

As soon as the chief's security men heard that he was being interrogated, they came out rushing with axes and big sticks. Suddenly they heard someone shouting.

"No! Put those axes and sticks down. Hands up!" one of the gangsters shouted, pointing a gun at them.

The rest of the gangsters came out from the car and started shooting the security men. They went in every room, shooting Chief Muyabwo's family from the youngest to the eldest. There was no mercy from the gangsters. Every member of Chief Muyabwo's family was crying for mercy, but nobody listened to their plea. The floor was covered in blood, and the brick walls were crying for air. Only the fittest could survive, because the victims were about to painfully drown in a blood pool.

"But how can you do this to me, Methuselah? At least you could have left my family alive," Chief Muyabwo pleaded.

"Well, when you killed my parents, you never felt sorry for them," Methuselah said. "Chief Muyabwo, today you are going to pay for your brutality. Your reign of brutality ends today! Sarowe villagers are free from brutality after today. Now, shoot the chief mercilessly!"

Immediately Chief Muyabwo was shot twice. One bullet went into his head, and one went into his chest. He fell down slowly with his dying breath, and blood came through his mouth.

"Oh! Oh, I am dead! I am dead!"

After he said his last words, he took his last breath and died. There was bloodshed everywhere, and so the gangsters and Methuselah drove off fast.

To date, nobody knows who shot Chief Muyabwo and his family.

ABOUT THE AUTHOR

Writing has always been my passion, and to fulfil this urge, I began writing short poems, some of which were published in 2004. I feel writing is an expression of inner feelings and is compassion to express how I feel from within. I have also published a novel called *Never Give Up*, a book based on true-life story, published in 2008. This book is my second book, and it is a fiction one. I have enjoyed writing this book so much, based on my own imagination and creativity. I feel great that I'm able to come up with such an amazing story.

CPSIA information can be obtained
at www.ICGtesting.com
Printed in the USA
FFHW021934150819
54326819-60002FF